Midnight Dancer

To Catch a Thief

They were nearly home when Mory was shaken out of her reverie by Aunt Olwen's sudden braking, which caused a clatter of pony feet from the trailer. A red motorbike skidded to a halt in front of them. The rider pushed the bike to the edge of the lane without a hint of apology. Aunt Olwen edged past.

"What a fool," she said. "He was going much too fast. That could have been nasty."

"I hope the ponies are all right," said Cara.

"It's Lionel's brother again," said Mory. "He's always round here. Do you think he's up to something?"

Midnight Dancer

To Catch a Thief

by Elizabeth Lindsay
illustrated by Linda Boddy

Hippo

Scholastic Children's Books,
Scholastic Publications Ltd,
7-9 Pratt Street, London NW1 0AE, UK

Scholastic Inc.,
730 Broadway, New York, NY 10003, USA

Scholastic Canada Ltd,
123 Newkirk Road, Richmond Hill,
Ontario, Canada L4C 3G5

Ashton Scholastic Pty Ltd,
P O Box 579, Gosford, New South Wales,
Australia

Ashton Scholastic Ltd,
Private Bag 1, Penrose, Auckland,
New Zealand

First published by Scholastic Publications Ltd, 1993

Text copyright © Elizabeth Lindsay 1993
Illustrations copyright © Linda Boddy, 1993

0 590 55137 X

Typeset by A J Latham Ltd, Dunstable
Printed by Cox & Wyman Ltd, Reading, Berks.

10 9 8 7 6 5 4 3 2 1

Contents

For Emily

ONE

First Steps

Mory held the end of the halter rope and stroked Midnight Dancer's neck. Stretching an arm across her withers, she let the pony take her weight. Dancer didn't seem to mind. The temptation to get on her for the first time was too much. Mory eased herself up, slid her leg over and gently sat. With a mewing cry a bird swooped across the sky. Startled, Dancer's head came up; her ears flattened. She leapt forward and bucked her way down the field, leaving Mory in a heap on the grass.

"Oh, hell's bells," said Mory, rubbing her hand where the rope had burned. "Mory Harper, sometimes you are so stupid." Dancer looked back, alert and magnificent. Mory got up and fished in her pocket for some pony nuts. The alarm didn't last long. By the time Mory reached her, Dancer was grazing as if nothing had happened.

"Here, girl," Mory said, picking up the halter rope before the pony trod on it. "That'll teach me to be impatient. But I'll be riding you soon. Wait and see." The pony gobbled up the nuts and nuzzled for more. "I promise not to sit on you again until you're really ready," she said, stroking the silky, black face.

"Mory, can you give me a hand?" shouted her father from the gate.

Mory slipped the halter over the pony's ears and let her go.

"Hurry up."

"I'm coming," Mory called and ran.

"There's never anyone around when I want them," said David.

"I'm around, Dad," said Mory.

"True," he said. Mory, grinning, followed David into the old henhouse which he was slowly turning into a pottery. The fact that it was slow was causing him a lot of frustration.

"What do you want me to do?" Mory asked, coming through the door and jumping into what seemed like a pit.

"Hold that for me," David said, giving her the end of a tape measure. "On the far wall. I've got to work out how many cubic metres of concrete I need for the floor." He wrote down the length. "Now the other way." Mory moved round and David noted the width. "I'm ordering it for the morning and I want everyone to help. The stuff goes hard really fast." Mory turned to go as David measured the depth.

"Hang on a sec. I need help spreading the polythene."

"But Dad, Cara's giving me a riding lesson."

"It'll only take a few minutes."

Mory resigned herself. "What polythene?"

"It lies under the concrete to stop the damp rising."

Mory spread the polythene while David paid out the roll. It was a long way from being the old henhouse it had been when they had first come to Black Rock Farm a few weeks before. The rotten inside had been gutted and David had dug out barrow loads of earth to make way for the concrete.

"Thanks, Mory," he said when they had finished. As Mory climbed out of the doorway David smiled. "No more climbing out after tomorrow," he said. "The floor will be level with the bottom of the door."

Mory knew how much her father wanted to start potting. He had a big order from a tea shop in Waring where they used to live and a shop in Covent Garden wanted pots for the tourist trade. He was longing to make them, just as she had longed to own Midnight Dancer.

They had lived at Black Rock Farm since the beginning of the Easter holidays and what Mory had thought she was going to hate she had begun to love. She ran out of the yard glad to have helped. She turned onto the track that led up to Llangabby Farm just as her mother drew up at the front gate.

"Check the letter box for me," Sheila called.

There were piles of shopping bags in the back of the car, including several rolls of chicken netting. Sheila had been to Aberdawl. Mory lifted the lid on the front of the box.

"Did you remember to post my letter to Hannah?" she asked as she handed the post through the car window,

"I certainly did," Sheila said. "Thanks, love. Lunch at one sharp. Tell Josh. I've got a lot to do this afternoon." With that her mother drove into the yard.

Mory set off up the track for Llangabby thinking of Hannah, her best friend. It had been dreadful leaving her behind in Waring. That was probably why she had been so stand-offish when they first came. The arrival of Midnight Dancer had changed

4

all that. Mory had glimpsed a black pony in the mist just after their arrival and later she had caught her. She had tried to explain her feelings to Hannah in the letter. The incredible excitement of it all; the disappointment at finding the pony belonged to Owen Lewis, a man who wanted them to pay an impossible thousand pounds for her; the despair when they lost Dancer in the Aberdawl pony sales to Caroline Spencer; the drama when they rescued Mr Lewis with his broken ankle and the joy when the Spencers finally sold Dancer to them.

Mory laughed, remembering her old self; the one not wanting to come; the one hating it when she got here. She was sorry now that she had been so grumpy with her cousin, Cara. They had never met before and Cara, Aunt Olwen and Uncle Glyn had been so welcoming when they arrived at Llangabby Farm. Cara and Josh had become friends at once. But then Josh had been looking forward to the new life, not back at the old as she had been.

Lucky Cara's forgiven me, thought Mory, kicking a stone. I think she understands.

Now Cara was teaching both Mory and Josh to ride. All three of them had ponies. Midnight Dancer was Mory's very own, Misty belonged to Cara, and Megan and Ian Reece who ran the Penyworlod Equestrian Centre had let Josh have Rustler, a lovely chestnut gelding, on six weeks' trial. Josh was hoping like mad that he could keep him.

The awfulness of nearly losing Dancer came flooding back. The anguish when Owen Lewis had put the pony in the auction and when Caroline Spencer's father had outbid them. But rescuing Mr Lewis had made everything come right. That and the fact that Caroline Spencer was obviously stupid with ponies. Mory couldn't stand the thought of her. Anyone who could make Dancer kick must be a real beast. Dancer, the kindest and gentlest of ponies. Nothing would ever make her like Caroline Spencer after that and she was glad she would never have to see her again. Mory kicked another stone, remembered her riding lesson and ran. She arrived in the Llangabby Farm yard puffed and smiling.

"Where've you been?" said Josh. "We're fed up with waiting."

"I've been helping Dad. Sorry."

"Guess what? I did a jump!" said Josh.

"You didn't!"

"He did," said Cara. "And lived. Rustler's in the stable."

Pulling on her hard hat, Mory went to fetch him. It was no good her trying to do a jump. She'd fall off. It was annoying that Josh was better than her. Try as she would, she couldn't catch up.

Up down, up down, up down, up down, Mory recited in her head as she trotted round the field on Rustler.

"Keep your hands still," ordered Cara. "And sit and canter." Mory did her best to follow the instructions. She sat, she bounced, she sort of asked with her legs and somehow Rustler cantered. One two three, one two three, one two three.

"Whoa," she said. "Whoa, boy."

"Sit up," said Cara. "Sit up, when you ask him to stop."

"It's no good," said Mory. "I'll never get it."

"Yes, you will. Stop trying so hard. Just relax and go with the movement. Trot round again. Remember to ask for the turn with the inside leg and inside hand. Keep a good contact with the outside rein. Go on."

Mory sighed and asked Rustler to walk. That was easy. If she could do everything at a walk, riding would be great.

"And trot," said Cara. "Come on."

Mory felt irritable.

"And canter." It was all very well for Cara, she could do it easily. Cara'd been riding for years and had had Misty for ages. Of course she was good. It wasn't fair.

"That's tons better," said Cara. "Tons better. You see you can do it."

For the first time she wasn't bouncing. Surprised, Mory stiffened and bounced at once, but she had done it.

"Lean back," shouted Cara. Mory leaned back, concentrated on relaxing into the movement and did it again. She sat, bottom on saddle, hips moving to the rhythm, while Rustler cantered. It felt wonderful.

"Well done," said Cara, clapping. She was as pleased as if she had done it herself.

The lesson over, Mory led Rustler to the gate. She put her hand in her pocket and Rustler wiggled his lips expectantly. Mory gave him a piece of carrot.

"Good boy," she said, patting him. He was hot.

"He's worked hard," said Cara. "Haven't you, boy? He could do with a good wash down."

"And after that we'll have to go, Josh," said Mory. "Mum said one sharp for lunch and you know what she's like if we're late. And tomorrow we've got to help Dad. The cement lorry's coming."

"Great," said Josh, who loved things like that.

"Thanks for the lesson," said Mory. "It was smashing."

"Hey," said Josh. "If it's quick-dry concrete we'd better watch we don't get our boots stuck."

"Trust you to think of that," said Mory.

They'd just finished washing down Rustler when a van drove past the yard and turned onto the track for Black Rock.

"I'll bring Misty down," said Cara.

"Eat with us, Cara," said Mory. "You might as well. I'll tell Aunt Olwen."

The van was in the yard when they got back and a man up a ladder was fixing something to the chimney stack. They turned Misty and Rustler out into the field with Dancer and went indoors.

"Cara's going to have lunch with us. Is that all right?" Mory said.

"Fine," said Sheila. "Put the cheese on the table, please, someone. And call Dad. Oh, and ask the aerial man if he wants a cup of tea."

"Hey, does that mean we can watch the telly?" cried Josh.

"I expect so."

"Great," said Josh. "I'll go and ask him."

"He says he doesn't expect we'll have fantastic reception as we live in a dip," warned Sheila. "And don't forget to call Dad." But Josh had already gone.

"I haven't missed the telly a bit," said Mory, unwrapping a lump of cheese.

"Wait for the long, cold winter evenings," said Sheila.

"I shall read books and draw pictures."

"I'll remember that when I'm trying to unglue you from the screen," Sheila laughed.

When lunch was over and they were clearing away the dishes, Sheila suddenly said, "Guess what? I bumped into Mr and Mrs Spencer and Caroline in Aberdawl." Mory stopped dead in her tracks. "They think they had an attempted burglary last night. They came back late to find a police car sitting in the drive and the burglar alarm ringing."

"Did the police see anyone?" Josh asked.

"No, they didn't. They think the alarm going off frightened whoever it was away."

"If it was a burglar," said Mory.

"Pretty suspicious," said Josh.

"Scary," said Cara.

"Anyway, they're having a house-warming party tomorrow evening and they've invited us."

"You didn't say we'd go?" said David.

"I said we'd be delighted."

"Mum!" Mory was horrified. "Caroline Spencer's foul."

"Don't worry. Children aren't invited," said Sheila. "It's a grown ups' party."

"I'm finishing the roof tomorrow," said David.

"A bit of socialising will do you good," said Sheila. "And the party won't stop you finishing anything."

"Oh, all right."

"Good, that's settled then."

The washing up continued in silence. Mory kept pulling faces behind Sheila's back and Josh kept giggling.

"That's enough, you two," said David. "Behave yourselves."

"You know what I think we should do, David?" said Sheila.

"Not go to the party," said Mory. Sheila ignored this.

"I think we should make you a temporary pottery in the cowshed. It wouldn't take long. You could start your orders while the concrete's drying out and not be so rushed later."

David paused with his drying up. "Sheila, that's brilliant. Why didn't I think of that?" He flung the tea towel at Josh and his arms around Sheila. Josh and Cara laughed. Mory hardly noticed.

She was thinking of Caroline Spencer turning up like a bad penny when she had hoped never to hear of her again. She wandered into the living room and found the sofa covered in shopping bags – school things. She remembered, with a sigh, that they started at Llantrist village school on Monday. Already the holidays were nearly over.

TWO

Traitors

The cement lorry arrived at eight-thirty the following morning with Uncle Glyn and Cara following in the Landrover. The Harper family were ready and waiting as it turned into the yard.

"Where do you want it?" the driver asked.

"Can you get it in here?" David indicated the pottery.

"Easy enough," said the driver.

He backed the lorry close to the pottery door and climbed out. The giant mixer turned. Inside, the concrete tumbled like an everlasting wave on a shingle beach. The driver pulled out a chute and tucked the end inside the doorway.

"Here goes," he said.

The mixer slowed, stopped and began to turn the other way. Concrete poured down the chute.

"Whoa," cried David, "We'd better shovel that lot over. It'll be coming out of the window in a minute."

"Okay," said the driver. "But I can't wait long, I've got another delivery."

David, Sheila and Uncle Glyn squeezed past the chute, slithered across the concrete and began to shovel.

"Can we come in?" Josh shouted.

"Not just yet," said Sheila.

"Honestly," said Mory, still irritated with her parents for accepting the Spencers' party invitation and not in the mood for hanging around. "What are we supposed to do?"

"Let's bring the ponies in," said Cara.

By the time the shovellers were ready for the rest of the concrete, Josh was receiving instruction in the driver's cab and the girls had gone.

"Shall we try lungeing today?" Mory asked, as she brushed Dancer's shiny coat. She'd been studying the book Megan Reece had lent her. She imagined Dancer trotting round her on the end of a long rein, obedient to her every command.

"First things first," said Cara. "She needs to get used to wearing a saddle and bridle."

"Right. Let's do the bridle," said Mory, going to fetch it.

Mr Lewis had given her the bridle and a saddle, a thank-you present for rescuing him. The bridle had an old snaffle bit, the sort with a bendy joint in the middle and big rings at the sides.

"We won't need the reins," said Cara. Mory undid them. "Go on then, put it on."

Mory held the bit in her left hand. She asked

Dancer to open her mouth by putting gentle pressure on Dancer's bottom jaw with a finger. Mory slipped the bit between Dancer's teeth and the headpiece over her ears. Dancer tried to spit the bit out but it wouldn't go.

"Poor Dancer, having that horrid cold piece of metal in her mouth," said Mory.

"She'll get used to it," said Cara as she adjusted the cheek pieces. "The bit's too big, really."

"I shall buy one the right size," said Mory, putting "new bit for Dancer" on her mental shopping list.

"Megan'll have one in her tack shop," said Cara. "Now, we'll leave the bridle on for about twenty minutes." Dancer fiddled, trying to get rid of the thing in her mouth. "We'll do it again tomorrow and the day after until she's happy with it, then we'll try her saddle on."

Mory remembered her useless attempt at sitting on Dancer. A saddle would accustom the pony to something on her back, something much less awkward than a person.

Shrieks from outside sent all three of them to the door. The lorry had gone and David was hosing down Josh's boots.

"Dad," cried Josh. "The water's gone in."

"Oh, dear, has it really?" said David, laughing.

"It's not funny," said Josh, grabbing the hose. He directed water down David's wellies.

"Gotcha!"

"That's enough," yelled David, jumping out of the way. "Mine was a genuine mistake." The girls, not ones to miss a chance, ran from the stable. Josh turned the hose on them. Mory dived for the hose-pipe. Soon there was a free-for-all with everyone screaming and yelling and getting wet.

At first Midnight Dancer backed into the stable, alarmed, but curiosity overcame her and she watched the water battle with fascination, her ears flicking backwards and forwards, ready to hide the moment any water sprayed her way. Nobody saw Splodge, Mory's cat, come into the yard. It was only when he was covered with a sudden gush that Mory yelled, "Stop!"

Splodge took flight, straight into the pottery. Realising his mistake, he came running out again, leaving behind a circle of little paw prints. Laughing, David turned off the tap.

"Well, the floor's been christened," he said. "A permanent memento to Splodge."

Uncle Glyn came into the yard. Sheila followed.

"Good grief," he said. "You're all wet."

Sheila looked grimly at the soaking foursome.

"Dad started it," said Josh. "He put water in my wellies."

"It was a mistake," said David, brushing a drip from his nose. "I was attacked."

"Just because you've finished the floor," said

Sheila. Mory looked. The pottery floor was as high as the door, with faint marks across it where it had been tapped level with the side of a plank and, of course, Splodge's little footprints.

"It looks great, Dad."

"It's a proper start," said David.

"Thanks for the tea, Sheila," said Uncle Glyn. "I'll take Cara up in the Landrover to change."

"Don't worry, Glyn, she can borrow some of Mory's clothes. All of you indoors and out of those wet things."

Before she went in, Mory took off Dancer's bridle. In the excitement Dancer seemed to have forgotten she was wearing it.

"You're a good girl," said Mory, giving her a handful of soggy pony nuts and a wet pat.

Mory brooded for the rest of the day on what was, she decided, her parents' disloyalty in going to the Spencers' party.

"Why've you got to go?" she asked as she watched her mother dress.

"We haven't got to go, we're going because we want to. It was nice to be asked. Can you do the zip, please?" Mory did up the zip, wondering why she felt so resentful. She watched Sheila sit in front of the dressing table and pull a brush through her hair.

"Are you going to wear Gran's necklace?" she asked.

"I think so. It goes nicely with this dress, don't you think?"

Sheila took out a black jewellery case. Inside the case was a necklace with a silver chain and two rows of real sapphires. Mory loved this necklace. First it had belonged to her great-grandmother, then her grandmother and now her mother. It was very old. Sheila called it the family heirloom. The stones, pale blue, reflected the light. It was dazzling. Mory lifted Sheila's hair and did up the clasp.

"The Spencers are very honoured," she said. Sheila laughed.

"Olwen is going to keep an eye on you all until we get back," she said.

"Can Cara stay the night?"

"If she wants."

David called from the bottom of the stairs.

"If we're going, let's go. At this rate it'll be time to come home before we've even started." Sheila picked up her handbag from the bed, plonked a kiss on Mory's cheek and hurried from the room. Slowly Mory closed the lid on the jewellery case.

From her bedroom window she watched her parents drive up the track. Rotten traitors, she thought. Her imagination, always vivid, saw Caroline, boasting with a smirk to the party guests about a horrid pony she'd had and how they'd had to sell it because it kicked.

"Oh, really," said Mory and went downstairs. She was moody all evening. In the end Cara went home rather than stay.

"What's up with her?" said Mory.

"What's up with you?" said Josh, going upstairs to bed.

"Well, I think they're traitors," said Mory defiantly.

"Who?" asked Aunt Olwen, looking up from her newspaper.

"Mum and Dad."

"I think you're being a bit over-dramatic."

"No, I'm not. Nobody understands, that's all."

In bed, Mory gazed at the three pictures of Dancer she had pastelled, still the centrepiece on her wall, and stroked Splodge, absentmindedly listening to his purr.

"Caroline Spencer could have ruined Dancer for life. Why can't anybody see that but me?" Splodge stretched a paw across the bed as if to say he could see perfectly well and would Mory please tickle him. Mory did so until he turned over and boxed her hand with his feet. She lifted him to the bottom of the bed and sighed.

"Night, night, Splodge." Splodge curled up and Mory put out the light.

The next morning was Sunday, the last day of the holidays. Cara found Mory in the stable grooming Dancer.

"Let's lunge Dancer now," Mory said, "and let her wear the bridle later."

"All right, if it'll make you happy."

Mory grinned. Cara put on the lungeing cavesson, the special noseband, with rings on either side and the front, offering a choice of place to fix the lungeing rein. Mory clipped the rein to the near side and led Dancer into the paddock behind the barn. Two faces, a grey and a chestnut, stared through the hedge.

"They always want to know what's going on," said Mory.

"Curiosity," said Cara. "If they upset Dancer we'll have to put them in."

Cara held Dancer while Mory arranged the lungeing rein in her left hand and the long lungeing whip in her right. She had learnt the theory but could she do it in practice? She held the whip still, pointing towards Dancer's hind quarters and the ground.

"Ask her to walk on," instructed Cara.

"Walk on," said Mory in an encouraging, clear voice. Cara led Dancer forward and round she went.

"Whoa," said Mory and Cara halted Dancer. They did this two or three times with Cara leading the pony. Then she let go.

"Walk on," commanded Mory. Dancer didn't move, so Mory lifted the whip. Dancer shot forward in a fast trot. "Steady girl. Walk. Whoa."

They tried again. This time Cara held Dancer while Mory gently raised the whip. She wanted to shoot off but Cara held her to a walk. After about ten minutes, she accepted the raising of the whip as a signal to go forward. They tried her going round the other way. Stopping, starting into a walk and stopping again. By the time they had finished, Dancer knew "walk on" and "whoa" and obeyed. Mory praised the pony and gave her an apple. Dancer chewed with relish. They turned her out with the others and Cara caught Misty.

"I'm going for a ride with Josh," she said. "Do you want to come?"

"No thanks," said Mory. "I'm going to help Dad today. It's my last chance to earn some money before school starts."

"I wish my dad paid a pound an hour," said Cara.

"I don't expect mine will once the pottery's finished."

The two girls went indoors. Josh was eating muesli and moaning about it and David was making scrambled eggs.

"Mory, take that mug of tea up to your mum, will you? Who wants scrambled eggs?" They all did.

In her parents' bedroom, Sheila lay curled up underneath the duvet. The black dress lay across the dressing table stool and the sapphire necklace hung on the corner of the mirror. Sheila stirred as Mory put the mug of tea on the bedside table.

"Thanks, love," she said.

"Dad's getting breakfast."

"That's nice of him," said Sheila, yawning. "Is that the time? Good heavens, I'd better get up."

Sheila came downstairs sipping her tea, and while the children finished breakfast she told them about the party. It had been mostly neighbours of the Spencers. A sort of getting-to-know-you party. The house was like a palace, full of antiques. It was difficult to move without fear of knocking some valuable piece over and the furniture was elegant but uncomfortable.

"I felt rather sorry for Caroline. I know she has everything she wants but somehow the house didn't feel as though a child lived in it. There was no trace of her."

"If only we could train our kids to be like that," said David. "They leave their junk everywhere."

"You'd have to give us everything we want," said Mory.

"Like Rustler," said Josh, getting in his request.

"The Spencers are funny people," Sheila went on. "They've bought Caroline a new pony. No expense spared, it seems."

"Of course," said Mory.

"But the surprising thing is they're sending her to the local school. I was sure they'd send her to a private one."

"You mean she's going to go to the same school as us?" said Josh.

"Bad luck," said David.

"Oh, no!" said Mory. The news put a blight on the rest of her day. Having Caroline Spencer at the same school was going to spoil everything. It was too bad.

THREE

School

Monday morning was chaos. Mory escaped by going to talk to Dancer. She stroked the pony's silky nose and gently pulled her ears. She had been looking forward to her new school but was less enthusiastic now that Caroline Spencer would be there. Her mother called, leaning indignantly over the gate.

"For goodness' sake, Mory, what do you think you're doing? We're ready to go."

The car bumped up the track. They drove out of the morning mist and into the farmyard at Llangabby to pick up Cara and Aunt Olwen.

"Sorry we're late," said Sheila.

The children were unusually silent as the car drove along the lane to the main road.

"Did you pick up your lunch box, Mory?" Sheila asked.

"Yes, Mum."

"And you, Josh?"

"You gave it to me."

25

"Did I?"

More silence. They overtook the school bus. Cara waved to some friends but they didn't see her.

They drove into Llantrist and past the village shop.

"Did I tell you? The shop was burgled a couple of days ago," said Aunt Olwen.

"How terrible," said Sheila.

"Took four days' takings, the thief did, and Mr and Mrs Pugh asleep upstairs. Makes you think you're not safe in your own bed these days."

"Have the police caught the thief?" Josh asked.

"They've no clues at all from what I've heard. Mrs Pugh said she thought she heard a motorbike drive through the village, that's all. Shocking, isn't it?"

"It might be the same thief that tried to rob the Spencers. Remember they told you about the burglar alarm going off," said Mory.

"It might be," said Sheila. "Even with the alarm it must be a worry with so many antiques around the house."

"That's the trouble with collecting valuables," said Aunt Olwen.

"They've some beautiful pieces of Sheraton," said Sheila. "Apparently, Mr Spencer is a well known expert."

"What's Sheraton?" Josh asked.

"It's a style of furniture made in the eighteenth century."

"They must have pots of money," said Mory.

"I heard they dealt in jewellery," said Aunt Olwen.

"Mrs Spencer's speciality."

"That's what I'd be worried about," said Aunt Olwen. "Easier to steal than furniture."

"Not this jewellery," said Sheila. "It's locked in a safe."

"Pots and pots of money," said Mory, thinking how nice that would be.

They followed the road past the churchyard and stopped by the church gate. The village primary school stood opposite, a Victorian building with an asphalt playground and small playing field beyond.

"It's got a football pitch," said Josh.

They hadn't seen the school before. They had arrived after the term had ended and had never been to Llantrist. All their shopping was done in Aberdawl which, though further, was a proper town with banks, supermarket and a cattle market where Uncle Glyn sold his sheep.

Mory had that strange lump-in-the-tummy feeling she got when she did something new.

"Careful as you cross the road," said Sheila.

The school bus arrived and its passengers tumbled out. Suddenly there was noise and bustle as children shouted and jostled. Mory was surprised by how few pupils there were. Hundreds had gone to her school in Waring. This was quite different.

They crossed the playground and followed Cara and Aunt Olwen into the school. Mory's school bag got caught in the door. As she turned to pull it out she caught a glimpse of Caroline Spencer coming through the gate and let the door close. She was not going to hold it open for that girl.

Inside the school was a small hall, an office, two cloakrooms for coats and two classrooms. That was all. The toilets were in the playground. All the juniors were in one classroom and all the infants in the other. This meant she would be in the same class as Josh. A novel experience for a term. After that she and Cara would be going to Aberdawl Comprehensive.

A woman, coming out of one of the classrooms, beamed a welcoming smile. Cara gave Mory a nudge.

"Mrs Morgan, how nice to see you," said the woman to Aunt Olwen. "You've brought our new pupils. Welcome, Morag and Joshua. I'm Mrs Wynne, your class teacher. I'm sure you'll be very happy here. Cara, show Morag and Joshua where to put their coats."

Mory and Josh followed Cara, leaving Sheila and Aunt Olwen talking to Mrs Wynne.

"She's here," said Mory under her breath.

"Who?" said Cara.

"Caroline Spencer. I saw her coming in the gate."

All the coat pegs had names. Mory found one saying Morag Harper.

"Do you think she'll let me change it?" Mory asked. She hated the name Morag.

"You can ask," said Cara. "Here's yours, Josh."

"Mrs Wynne seems okay," said Josh.

"She is," said Cara. "She's really nice."

"Everything all right?" Sheila asked.

"Fine," said Mory.

"We'll be off, then. Enjoy yourselves."

In the hall, Mrs Wynne was talking to Mr and Mrs Spencer. Caroline stood by, swinging a pink bag. Mory followed Cara and Josh into the classroom. Children were milling about, sitting and standing, chatting and laughing, mostly swapping stories about the holidays. A woman in an overall came over to them.

"This is Mrs Price," said Cara.

"Hello, Cara," said Mrs Price. "These two new faces must be your cousins?"

"I'm Mory," said Mory quickly before Mrs Price could say Morag. "And this is Josh."

"You're going to be on Cara's table," said Mrs Price to Mory. "And you, Josh, come with me. You're over here. Steven Evans, I want you a minute."

"Who's she?" Mory asked, as Josh trailed after her.

"Mrs Wynne's assistant. She's not a teacher. She helps."

Mrs Wynne popped her head around the door.

"Cara, come here please," she called. Mory sat at her place and felt shy. Two boys were chatting together. It left three places, one of which was Cara's. The windows were so high that she couldn't see out. It was all so different from her other school, where the building had been modern and bright. The boys started giggling. Mory turned away in case they were giggling at her, to find Cara leading Caroline Spencer across the classroom.

"Oh, no," Mory groaned.

"This is your place," said Cara, indicating an empty chair, next to the boys.

"It's a bit poky in here," said Caroline, plonking the pink bag on the table. "Not at all like my last school."

"This is Gareth and this is Lionel," said Cara.

"Watcha," said Gareth, grinning. Lionel, a redhead, didn't look up. Mory surveyed his pink skin and brown freckles and wondered if he was pink from embarrassment or whether he was always like that. Observing him more closely she saw his shirt had a torn sleeve and was rather grubby.

"Sarah Williams is on this table too but Mrs Price says she's ill. Sarah's got a pony and Lionel rides too."

Cara had meant this information for Mory but it was Caroline who said in sharp, clear tones, "I've got a super new pony. It does everything. Much better than the first one I had, which was useless."

Cara was struck dumb. The boys giggled and Mory felt a surge of rage. Luckily Mrs Wynne chose that moment to clap her hands for silence.

"We're going to have an assembly with the infants," she said. "We've new people to welcome today. Stand quietly and when everyone's ready, Mrs Pugh will ask you to lead into the hall." And so the first day at school began.

Mory ignored Caroline for the rest of the morning. Blotting her out, she concentrated on work. The trouble began at lunchtime. It rained and so they stayed indoors. Mory had finished her sandwiches and was putting her lunch box away when Caroline came marching over.

"You're the girl who's got my pony, aren't you? I knew I'd seen you somewhere before. You were at the auction that time when Daddy bought her for me."

"She's not your pony," said Mory. "She's mine."

"She's a nasty, bad-tempered thing," said Caroline. "She kicked me."

"Good for her," said Mory. "I hope it hurt." Lionel giggled.

"What did you say?" said Caroline.

"You heard." Mory turned away and zipped up her bag. For a moment Caroline was at a loss, but only for a moment.

"Too poor to buy her at the auction, weren't you? You could only afford a cheap dud!"

Mory whipped round, glaring.

"Don't," Cara whispered. "It's not worth it."

With an effort Mory controlled herself and shrugged.

"Think what you like," she said and turned back to her bag. She wanted to say more. She wanted to say a lot more. But Cara was right. It wasn't worth it. There were other ways to show Caroline Spencer how good Dancer was. She'd show her by riding better than Caroline could ever ride.

Caroline raised her chin, tauntingly.

"I don't suppose you've even sat on her yet. You wouldn't dare." This was almost too much for Mory, but Lionel, interest overcoming his shyness, saved the day.

"What's the matter with her?"

"Nothing," said Cara. "She's not broken in yet. We've just started lungeing her, that's all."

"Lucky you," Lionel said. "I want to be a trainer. Can I see her sometime?"

"Yes," said Mory. "Yes, of course you can. Anytime. Where do you live?"

"Not far. I got a bike. Sometimes Dad goes to Llangabby with hens. Maybe go with him."

"I shouldn't bother, if I were you," said Caroline. "Come and see my new pony, she's much better." But Lionel had already said too much. Blushing, he joined his friend Gareth at the computer.

"What's up with him?" said Caroline, pouting, and she flounced off to annoy Mrs Price, who was doing cutting out with some younger children.

"Phew!" said Mory.

"Double phew," said Cara. "I thought you were going to let her have it."

"I nearly did," said Mory.

When school finished they collected their coats, slung their bags over their shoulders and waited for the school bus. Caroline was met by her father. She shrugged off the arm he put around her shoulder and said something that made him look at the waiting children.

It came on to drizzle. Mory put up her anorak hood.

"Is the bus always late?" she asked.

"Hardly ever."

"Just our luck, then."

A bicycle rattled down the step from the playground. It was Lionel, his red hair tousled, looking miserable. He wiped an arm across his face as a motorbike roared into the village and purred to a halt beside him, its rider shrouded in black, the bike a gleaming red.

"What's up with Lionel?" Mory said.

"I expect Gareth's bashed him up again," said Cara.

"You said they were friends."

"They are most of the time."

"Some friend."

The man on the motorbike pulled off his helmet. His hair, the same colour as Lionel's, was long on top and shaved round the sides. He wore a large earring in his left ear. Grinning, he said something. Lionel didn't reply and was cuffed contemptuously around the head.

"Leave him alone, you bully!" Mory shouted. The man, looking round, surveyed the waiting children. Taking his opportunity, Lionel scurried into the road and pedalled off. It was quite clear who had shouted. Mory was glaring. The man pulled on his crash helmet and started the motorbike. The engine roared into life and he drove straight at her, swerving only at the last minute before speeding off.

"Fat thug!" shouted Mory, shaking her fist.

"Who's he?" said Josh, shaken.

"Lionel's brother," said Cara. "You took a chance, Mory."

"What a pig," said Mory.

The bus arrived and they climbed aboard. Finding seats, they sat down with a jolt as the bus accelerated.

"What's Lionel's pony like?" Mory asked.

"He hasn't got one," said Cara. "He works for the Reeces and rides theirs."

"But if he's so keen?"

"His dad won't let him have one, that's why. You saw what his brother was like, well, his dad's just the same."

"Doesn't his mum have any say?"

"She died," said Cara.

Rain beat against the window. Mory rubbed the condensation off and looked out.

"Poor Lionel."

Soon the bus stopped at the end of their lane and the three of them climbed out into the wet.

"Welsh weather," Mory grumbled.

They hadn't gone far when a motorbike raced up

behind them, going dangerously fast for such a narrow lane, forcing them to flatten themselves against the hedge.

"Stupid idiot," yelled Mory.

"He won't hear," said Josh.

"It's Royden, again. Lionel's brother," said Cara. "What does he think he's doing?"

A large wooden box strapped to the carrier on the back wobbled precariously as the bike disappeared round the bend, leaving an acrid smell of exhaust fumes. But when they turned into the farmyard at Llangabby, there was no sign of the motorbike or Royden.

"He wouldn't have gone down to us, would he?" Mory said.

"Weird," said Cara. "It looks like he's gone into the hills."

"Must be mad in this weather," said Mory.

"I wonder what's in the box?" said Josh.

"Who knows," said Mory. "Let's go home before we get soaked. See you, Cara." And, hunching into the rain, she set off down the track to Black Rock. Josh waved goodbye and followed. Cara hurried indoors.

FOUR
Lessons

Over the next few days, Mory had lessons at school and Dancer had lessons at home. Mory was up early each morning training Dancer on the lungeing rein. After school Dancer wore her bridle and, towards the end of the week, her saddle.

The first time Mory put the saddle on, Josh helped. He held Dancer's head while Mory gently lowered the saddle into place. Dancer was wary at first and put her ears back.

"It's all right, girl," Mory said reassuringly. "It's only a saddle." Slowly Mory reached for the girth and gently fastened it. She stroked the pony's neck.

"Good girl," she said. "Good girl." Dancer was rewarded with a titbit and left to familiarise herself with this new piece of tack.

"When are you going to get on her?" Josh asked.

"Soon," said Mory. "When she's ready."

Dancer seemed ready now. There she was, calmly looking over the stable door as if to say, "I've got used to the saddle. How much longer am I going to be stuck in here?"

By the weekend, Dancer was working fully tacked up with saddle, bridle and loose side reins made of bailer twine attached to the bit rings at one end and to the saddle at the other.

"You've done really well," Cara said, impressed.

"It's Dancer. She does what you ask."

"Then it's both of you. Remember what happened to Caroline. Dancer kicked her."

"Don't remind me."

Mory pulled a face. At school she'd spent the whole week biting her tongue at Caroline's persistent jibes. Mory's hope was that if she ignored them they would eventually stop. She led Dancer into the stable.

"Caroline's jealous," said Cara.

"Why? She doesn't need to be. She's got Wonder Pony, she keeps telling us."

"That's the give-away," said Cara. "Let's face it. You're making a success of Dancer and she didn't. It makes her look pretty stupid. She boasts to cover up."

"Maybe," said Mory. "I just wish she'd stop making snide remarks."

"She will. She'll have to in the end. Dancer's going to be really good."

"I hope so," said Mory.

"Anyway," said Cara with an impish grin, "you're going to get the chance to see Wonder Pony this afternoon. Caroline's joining our lesson at the Reeces'."

"Hell's bells! It'd better be as good as she says it is, that's all."

Mory led Dancer into the stable.

"Try leaning over her," suggested Cara. "Put a bit of weight on her back."

"I did that yesterday," said Mory. "She was fine."

"Okay, do that first and then you can do it using the stirrup to get all your weight on her."

Cara held Dancer's head while Mory leaned gently over her, first from one side, then the other. Dancer was so unconcerned that she nuzzled Cara's pocket for a treat.

"Now put your foot in the stirrup and lean right over," Cara said. Mory lowered the stirrup and put her foot in it. Slowly, transferring her weight to the stirrup, she leaned over the saddle. Dancer wasn't at all frightened.

"This is practically sitting on her," Mory said. "Good girl." She eased herself off.

"One more time," said Cara. Mory did the same again. "Stay there," Cara said. "Come on, Dancer. Walk on."

Cara led the pony slowly round the stable. Dancer was carrying Mory for the first time, even if it was like a piece of baggage.

"Whoa," said Cara. Mory slid off.

"Good girl," she said. "Good girl." Her eyes were alight. "You're fantastic." Dancer gobbled up the pony nuts offered and nuzzled for more.

"You'll be riding her soon," said Cara.

"I know." Mory was overjoyed. She turned Dancer out into the field and reported to David, who had a list of things for her to do.

Mory was humping a plank of wood from the cowshed to the pottery when a large grey van drove into the yard, stopping abruptly. The driver climbed out and inspected the nearside wing.

"Got a problem?" David asked.

"Some flipping lunatic on a motorbike. I just missed him and clipped the wall. At the top of the track it was."

"Did you get his number?"

"Didn't get a chance. A red bike, it was."

Sounds like Lionel's brother, thought Mory. Again. She dumped the plank in the pottery and went back for another.

"It's just the paint," said David.

"Lucky," said the driver. "I've come about the phone."

"Good," said David. "When are we getting it?"

"We're going to wire you up inside today. The fellas start putting up poles on Monday. It depends how they get on. By Wednesday, with luck."

"Great," said David. "A link with the outside world at last." The man laughed.

"It's a bit remote here, that's for sure," he said. "I wouldn't fancy this in the middle of a snowstorm."

Mory was fetching the last plank when Josh shouted for her.

"We're taking the ponies up to Llangabby. Can you bring the hard hats?"

"I'm off for the lesson now, Dad," said Mory, going into the cowshed. "Hey, that's the electric wheel."

"I've done some clever things with the power," said David. "Just don't tell the electricity board." Mory stepped over a confusion of cables.

"Has Mum checked the wiring?"

"Yes, as it happens, so you can stop worrying."

Sheila was good at things to do with electricity. That came from being a science teacher. Mory didn't trust David since the time he blew up her hairdryer.

Rustler and Misty clattered across the yard, led by Josh and Cara. Mory ran to fetch the riding hats. It wouldn't be long before she would be taking Dancer. Uncle Glyn had assured her there was room for three ponies in the trailer.

"Have a nice time," said Sheila when Mory dashed into the kitchen.

"Thanks, Mum. See you." Grabbing the hats, Mory raced to catch up with the others, just missing the telephone engineer on his way in.

LESSONS

When the Landrover drove into the Penyworld Equestrian Centre, Mory felt a stab of excitement. She was looking forward to the lesson, eager to learn, wanting to ride as well as she could.

Today she was going to have her lesson on one of the Reeces' ponies. Which pony would it be? Nothing would be as good as Dancer, she was sure of that. Aunt Olwen parked and everyone jumped out.

Josh and Cara led Misty and Rustler to the outdoor school. There was no sign of Caroline Spencer. Mory saw Lionel pushing a wheelbarrow to the dung heap and waved. He came over when he saw them.

"Ian says to tell you Megan won't be long. She's had to go to the Spencers' place. Caroline's pony wouldn't load."

Lionel went back to the wheelbarrow. Giving the message had turned him bright pink.

"Not such a perfect pony after all," said Mory. She walked to the stables, leaving Cara and Josh to warm up their ponies in the outdoor school, and found Ian in the tack room.

"Hello, Mory," he said. "We've put you down for Doughnut. I've left you to tack her up. Give you a chance to get to know her." He handed Mory a saddle and bridle. "Her name's on the door."

Mory walked down the row of loose boxes looking for Doughnut's stable. When she found it she said hello to the pony and went in. By the time she and Doughnut joined the others, Megan had returned.

"Come along, Mory," she said. "Let's get started. Caroline can join us when she's sorted herself out."

The lesson began. Walking, trotting and cantering. Mory found it all much easier now and Doughnut, though not as responsive as either Misty or Rustler, was willing enough. They were having a break, while Megan and Lionel laid out some poles for the ponies to trot over, when Caroline led a bright bay pony across to the school.

"Crumbs," said Cara. "It's a proper show pony. It must have cost a fortune." The pony was alert, graceful and slender limbed.

"It's like a miniature thoroughbred," said Lionel, undisguised admiration on his face.

Not only did Caroline have a new pony, it had a new saddle and bridle. Caroline was wearing smart breeches with black boots, an expensive hacking jacket and velvet hard hat. Mory looked down at her jeans and wellington boots. Not very elegant by comparison.

"Well, too bad," she thought.

"Bring him in, Caroline," said Megan. "Lionel, open the gate, please." Smiling proudly, Mr Spencer joined Aunt Olwen.

"He seems to have calmed down a bit after all that fuss," said Megan. "I forgot to ask you what he's called."

"Elveston Tawney," said Caroline.

"What do you call him for short?" Megan asked.

"Bert," suggested Mory. The others giggled.

Caroline ignored them and said, "He likes Tawney best."

Megan helped Caroline mount. When Megan let go, Tawney took it into his head to jog across the school towards the other ponies.

"Stop, you beast," said Caroline, pulling at the reins. The pony pulled back, yanking Caroline forward. Taking advantage of her state of unbalance, he put in a buck. Caroline flew over his shoulder and landed in a heap. Tawney, having deposited his rider on the ground, trotted to Doughnut to say hello.

Megan helped Caroline up and made sure she wasn't hurt. Lionel quickly caught Tawney before he caused any more trouble, while Megan helped Caroline brush the sand off her jacket.

"Have you ridden Tawney before?" Megan asked.

"No," said Caroline. "Daddy said I wasn't to until I came here."

"Would you mind very much if I asked Lionel to ride him for a few minutes to get some of the bounce out of him? Lionel, fetch a hat."

"No," said Caroline, pouting. What she really wanted to say was yes, she did mind, but she didn't dare. Besides, she didn't feel like getting on again just at the moment.

"Looks like they've managed to get another pony that won't do," said Josh.

Lionel came running back with a hat, blushing profusely. His embarrassment vanished the moment he sat on Tawney. Gathering up the reins, he asked for a walk. The pony jogged. Lionel didn't seem to do much except talk to the pony and after a few more capers the pony did as it was asked. Lionel made it look its best, for after the first few strides when it resisted, the pony flexed its neck elegantly and moved forward into a free-striding walk. Lionel was really good. Ponies didn't just do that by themselves, Mory had already found that out.

"What have you been feeding him?" Megan asked.

"Oats and bran," said Caroline. "That's right, isn't it?"

"From now on, you must give him nothing but grass and if he gets any fatter that must be rationed too."

"But . . . "

"You do want to be able to ride him?"

"Yes," said Caroline earnestly. "I do."

"Oats will make him behave like a racehorse. That's no good to him or you. Grass will be quite adequate. Lionel, ask him to trot."

Walking and trotting, trotting and cantering, whatever Lionel asked for the pony did and did it willingly.

The interesting thing is, thought Mory, that Lionel makes it look so easy. Cara gave Mory a what-do-you-think-of-that look. Mory felt humbled. She wanted to be able to ride like Lionel more than anything.

When the time came for Caroline to re-mount, she looked apprehensive but bravely climbed on. The pony didn't look so good or go so well with Caroline riding but it didn't buck again and the lesson was able to continue.

"Thanks Lionel," said Megan. "Nicely ridden." Lionel glowed pink.

It was clear that Caroline was far from safe on Elveston Tawney. At the end of the lesson, Megan told her she was only to ride Tawney in the field at home. Mr Spencer nodded and Caroline agreed.

"What she really wants to do is show off," said Mory.

"Now, now, Mory," said Aunt Olwen.

Megan sent them home with words of praise ringing in their ears. It was true. They had all improved, including Caroline. Mory settled into the Landrover and happily daydreamed of riding Dancer.

They were nearly home when she was shaken out of her reverie by Aunt Olwen's sudden braking, which caused a clatter of pony feet from the trailer. A red motorbike skidded to a halt in front of them. The rider pushed the bike to the edge of the lane without a hint of apology. Aunt Olwen edged past.

"What a fool," she said. "He was going much too fast. That could have been nasty."

"I hope the ponies are all right," said Cara.

"It's Lionel's brother again," said Mory. "He's always round here. Do you think he's up to something?"

"Like what?" asked Josh.

"I don't know but we could follow him and see."

"We'd never keep up," said Cara.

"We'll follow his bike tracks then," said Mory. "Let's, when we get the chance."

FIVE

Tracks

The rest of the weekend flew by. Monday arrived and Mory found herself trudging along the lane with Cara and Josh to catch the school bus. It wasn't until she saw Lionel in the playground that she remembered Lionel's brother, Royden, but the sight of Caroline with her arm in a sling was much more interesting.

"What happened to you?" Mory asked, not unkindly.

"Mind your own business," Caroline replied.

"Don't tell me, you fell off Tawney again."

Caroline's eyes filled with tears. She pushed past and went into school.

"Don't, Mory. She's upset," said Cara.

"I only asked."

Sitting down at her place, Mory noticed one of Lionel's ears was swollen bright red. His eyes were puffy with dark rings under them and he was so dishevelled he might have been to bed in his clothes. Another fight? Mory wondered. Caroline dropped her pink bag. It was difficult to manage with one hand.

"I'll do it," said Mory, reaching for the bag.

"No," said Caroline, pulling it away. "Leave it alone."

"Look," said Mory. "I'm sorry I said what I said. I didn't mean to upset you."

"You're not a bit sorry," said Caroline, her voice rising. "You're glad I fell off." She burst into tears and rushed out, banging the classroom door. A deathly silence descended.

"Mory, come here please," said Mrs Wynne. "Would you mind telling me what that was all about?"

"I asked Caroline if I could help her with her bag and she said no. Then I said I was sorry for what I said in the playground."

"Which was?"

Mory looked at her feet.

"I asked if she'd fallen off her pony again."

Mory felt all eyes upon her. Mrs Wynne didn't say anything for ages. It was horrible.

"Go and sit down," she said at last.

Lessons began and still Caroline didn't come back.

"You've done it now," whispered Cara. The room was unusually quiet.

"I didn't do anything," said Mory. " I really tried to help and I apologised for what I said." It was too bad. Typical of Caroline to make a mountain out of a molehill. Mrs Wynne left the classroom. Mory was glum. Caroline was always digging at her about Dancer. She'd said one rotten thing and she'd apologised for it. Now she was blamed for upsetting Caroline. How unfair. Sarah Williams, who had been ill for a week, was wide-eyed.

Cara gave Mory a nudge. Lionel was lying with his head on his arm, sound asleep. Sarah leaned across and gave him a dig with her pencil. Lionel didn't stir. Mrs Wynne came back, leading Caroline by the hand. Sarah gave Lionel an extra-hard dig. He woke with a start and rubbed his arm. Confused, he stared at his exercise book as if he didn't know where he was.

"Caroline accepts your apology, Mory, so we'll say no more about it," said Mrs Wynne. Caroline sat down. "Are you all right, Lionel?" Lionel nodded.

Mory didn't look up. She was furious with Caroline for making such a fuss.

The day wore on. At lunchtime they sat out on the tarmac and ate their sandwiches in the sun. As it was the first time Sarah had been at school, Cara and Mory had lots to talk to her about. Josh played with his own friends on the football field. Caroline stayed in the classroom.

Not far from them, Lionel and Gareth were playing marbles. Lionel was losing. Gareth called him carrot tops. He didn't respond.

"Who's got a cauliflower ear, then?" Gareth
shouted. At which point Lionel lost his temper and
lashed out.

Soon the boys were punching and kicking, Lionel
yelling that Gareth was a cheat and a liar. Other
boys cheered until Mrs Pugh blew her whistle and
pulled them apart. The two combatants stood puff-
ing and glaring at each other. Lionel's nose dripped
blood. Mrs Pugh took Lionel indoors and Gareth
was left to look for the scattered marbles.

"Honestly," said Sarah. "Boys."

Mory said nothing. She admired Lionel for standing up for himself, particularly as he had no chance of winning against Gareth, who was bigger and stronger. The scene outside school on the first day played itself in Mory's head. Lionel's brother, Royden, taking off his crash helmet. Lionel coming out of school crying. His brother clipping Lionel round the head. Lionel was always being thumped and now he had a swollen nose to add to his swollen ear.

"What does Lionel's brother do?" she asked.

"Nothing," said Sarah. "His dad kicked him out last week. He said he wasn't having a hippy layabout spongeing off him."

"Where's he living now?" Cara asked.

"Don't know."

When school finished, Mory made a point of going over to Lionel in the cloakroom. He backed away when she approached. But when Mory talked about Megan and Ian Reece, Lionel forgot to be shy. Megan had taught him to ride, he said. He worked there as often as he could in return for lessons.

"I'm schooling Tawney for them."

"Are you?"

"He bucked her off again. They've lent Doughnut." No wonder Caroline was so touchy about her arm.

"You rode Tawney really well."

"The best ever, he is," said Lionel.

"Are you coming to see Dancer?"

"If I can." Lionel looked uncomfortable. "It's a bit tricky at the moment. My dad. . ." He swung his carrier bag. "I got to go. See you."

Towards the end of the week, things were a bit calmer. Caroline had abandoned the sling and Mory was careful not to mention anything about ponies in her presence. Caroline said nothing about swopping Tawney for Doughnut and Mory didn't let on that she knew.

The bombshell came on Friday morning at school assembly when Mrs Wynne announced that the school had been burgled the night before. There was a gasp from her listeners. Someone had broken into the office and taken the school fund cash box. The break-in was not as serious as it might have been. Apart from a broken window and a forced cupboard lock there was no damage.

"The thief knew exactly what he was looking for and where it was kept," she said.

Mory, who was as shocked as anyone, was standing next to Lionel. He seemed particularly upset. He wiped his nose on his sleeve and there were tears in his eyes.

"Luckily I'd just paid most of the fund money into the bank, so the school is only about ten pounds the poorer. I want you all to be extra vigilant. If you see or hear anything suspicious, tell me or your parents at once."

The school buzzed with the news and nothing else was talked of all day. It was hard to concentrate on lessons. Before she let them go home, Mrs Wynne announced that they were going to start a school project the following week.

"I want you to spend a little time looking for a stone, any sort of stone you like. You might choose it because of its shape or colour or its size. Bring the stone with you to school on Monday. It'll be interesting to see how many different stones we get. Don't forget."

"A stone!" said Mory under her breath, raising her eyebrows. "What for?"

Mrs Wynne dismissed them and they rushed to the waiting bus.

Once home, Cara went straight indoors to tell about the burglary and Mory and Josh ran to Black Rock and did the same.

"I thought we'd left all this sort of thing behind in Surrey," said Sheila.

"Just shows you it's no safer in the country," said David.

"We must lock up before we go out," said Sheila. "We've got very slack about remembering."

"You're right," said David. "But there's someone here most of the time. I don't think we need worry."

*

TO CATCH A THIEF

The following morning, Mory was up early. She pulled on her clothes and hurried downstairs with Splodge. Everyone else was fast asleep. She let Splodge out and put his breakfast in the back porch. Grabbing her hard hat, she went outside.

It was the perfect morning for a ride. She'd go on Rustler. Not far, just a little way into the hills. A sort of practice for when she could do the real thing on Dancer. She grabbed a halter and ran to the field. Dancer followed Mory and Rustler to the gate as if to say, "Take me. I want to go too."

"Don't worry, it'll be your turn soon enough," said Mory.

Dancer watched her lead Rustler into the stable. Rustler was tacked up and ready to go in no time. Mory led him through the yard and onto the track.

"Steady, boy," she said. She did up his girth and mounted. They didn't go up the track as Rustler expected; they went down. Where the track ran out, Mory turned onto a sheep path, hoping it would take them to the top of the ridge that sheltered Black Rock. There she could join the track that led into the hills from the end of the lane. The path opened out and Mory asked Rustler to trot. He wanted to go faster but Mory held him back. He was fresh and full of energy.

Mory reached the ridge and slowed to a walk. She was riding so much better now. She felt in control and confident. Looking back, Black Rock

was almost hidden in the dip below. They joined the track where wheel marks scored the ground, brown parallel lines weaving through the heather, up and over and out of sight. Trotting on, Mory followed the tracks for a while. Some were a criss-cross pattern of motorbike tracks. The going was good so Mory let Rustler canter.

They reached the summit of the hill. Here Mory slowed. The track dipped away and she didn't think she could manage cantering downhill. Rustler pulled to go on but Mory turned him. As she did so, she saw that the motorbike tracks led off to the right, down a narrower stony path.

So they didn't lead to old Mr Lewis's cottage as she had thought. Old Mr Lewis had owned Dancer until he died and, although his cottage was for sale, no one had bought it yet.

"Too remote," David had said. "With no mains electricity or piped water. It'll be a spartan person who wants to live there."

Mory had come to the limit of her exploration for today. They followed the bike tracks back the way they had come to Llangabby Farm. Rustler thought he was going into the farmyard until Mory turned him down the track for home.

They hadn't gone far when, in the distance, Mory heard a motorbike engine vibrate through the stillness of the morning. She turned the pony back up the track and into the farmyard. Dismounting quickly she tucked herself and Rustler behind the wall. She peeped out in time to see a red motorbike bounce down the track from the hills. Rustler started as the bike flashed by, the rider in black hunched over the handlebars, a big box on the back. Mory recognised Royden Jones easily enough.

"Steady, steady now," Mory said, stroking Rustler's neck. She mounted and set off again for Black Rock.

Back home, Mory led Rustler into a stable to untack him. She thanked him with a handful of pony nuts and turned him out with his friends in the field.

"Good boy," she said, patting him.

Mory found David and Josh in the kitchen having breakfast.

"Where've you been?" asked David.

"For a ride."

"On Rustler?" said Josh. "You never asked."

"You were asleep and anyway we're supposed to be sharing him until I can ride Dancer."

Josh looked upset. "You should've asked. You wouldn't like it if I went off with Dancer."

"Sorry, I will ask next time."

"You'd better," said Josh.

"And where did you go on this ride?" David asked. "I don't want you riding out into the hills and getting lost."

"Not far. I went round in a circle."

Before she could be cross-examined any further, the telephone rang.

"Hey, it's working," said Mory.

"Since yesterday," said David. He picked up the receiver. "Hello. Yes, hang on a minute. It's Cara for you." He handed Mory the phone.

"Hello. Really? A show? Bring it down now. Bye." Mory hung up. "It's great now we're on the phone, isn't it?"

"If you don't have to pay the bill."

"Oh, Dad!"

Mory and Josh met Cara in the yard. She waved the pony show schedule she'd rung up about.

"Megan and Ian are running it at Penyworlod." Cara was very excited. "It's at half term. I didn't think there'd be any local shows until the summer holidays." She was really pleased.

"What are you going to go in for?" Mory asked.

"There are two jumping classes and a dressage class and the pairs jumping if Josh will do it with me."

"Me?" said Josh. "But I've only jumped six times in my life."

"You've got till half term to practise," said Cara. "The jumps won't be very big."

"Well, if you think I can do it."

"And you can do the dressage."

"What's this Handy Pony class?" Mory asked.

"And we can do that," said Cara, beaming.

"But what is it?"

"You have to do various things like pick up and carry a big bag or ride your pony under a clothes line. Perhaps go over a small jump or drop a ball in a bucket. Silly things, but if your pony doesn't stop when you ask it, or shies at things like bags, you can't do it. It's to show how good your pony is. The fastest one round wins."

"That sounds all right," said Josh. "Rustler and I can manage that."

"What about Dancer? Will she be able to go in the Handy Pony?"

"It's a bit soon," said Cara. "I'd wait. After all,

you haven't ridden her yet. You don't really know what she's going to be like."

Cara folded up the schedule and put it in her pocket.

"Guess what I did this morning?" said Mory. "Followed bike tracks."

"So that's what you were up to," said Josh.

"I went along the ridge to where they turned off. Coming back, Royden came along the track from the hills."

"Did he see you?" Cara asked.

"No, I ducked into the yard before he came by. He made Rustler jump he was going so fast."

"Do you think he's living up there somewhere?" said Cara. "Since he got thrown out of home?"

"I thought he might be using old Mr Lewis's cottage but the tracks don't lead there."

"Well, he's up and down here a lot all of a sudden," said Cara. "You can't help noticing the row he makes on his bike."

"Yes," said Mory. "And if he isn't going to old Mr Lewis's cottage, where is he going to? I want to know." But she didn't want to be caught trying to find out. She didn't think Royden would take kindly to being spied on.

SIX

Riding Dancer

"Today's the day," said Cara, grinning.

"Yup," agreed Mory.

"You going to sit on Dancer?" Josh asked. "It's a historic moment! I'll tell Mum and Dad and I'll get my camera."

They gathered in the field behind the barn, the family and Dancer. Mory lunged Dancer one way and then the other. The pony went beautifully. Josh took a photograph while Sheila and David watched from the gate.

"Now, Mory, be careful," warned Sheila.

"She'll be fine, you'll see. Whoa, Dancer," said Mory, gathering up the lungeing rein. She undid the lungeing cavesson and took it off.

"Now we'll do all the things we've done before," said Cara.

Mory put her foot in the stirrup and leaned her weight on Dancer's back. Cara led Dancer forward. Walk and halt, walk and halt. Mory slid off.

"Keep perfectly relaxed," said Cara. "This time

when you put your foot in the stirrup get on properly."

Cara held the reins and the off-side stirrup leather. Mory put her foot in the stirrup and transferred her weight. Lifting her leg over Dancer's back she sat gently in the saddle. Dancer's ears flicked as if to say, this is a bit different. Josh took a photograph. Mory got off and got on and got off and got on.

"Let's go for a little walk," said Cara. Very gently, Mory gathered up the reins as Cara led Dancer forward.

"Good girl," said Mory, sitting as still as she could. "Good girl."

"Whoa," said Cara. The pony stopped. "Well, what do you think of that, eh, Dancer?" Cara gave Dancer a handful of pony nuts. Carefully, Mory dismounted.

"As good as gold," she said. "I knew she would be."

Sheila and David came and gave Dancer a pat.

"Well done, Mory," said Sheila. "Well done to your assistants, too."

"And well done, Dancer," said Mory, glowing with pride.

"Yes," said David. "Well done, Dancer. You were right, Mory, you've got a good 'un there."

"Well," said Sheila. "I would never have believed she'd be so placid."

"Proper preparation," said David. Cara grinned.

"Yes, I think she knew what to expect," she said. "Don't forget, seeing us ride the others will have helped too."

"What was it like?" Josh asked.

"I forgot to notice," said Mory. "I was concentrating on Dancer."

"If you do a bit each day, by next weekend we should be able to take her out for a short ride," said Cara.

"She hasn't got any shoes," said Mory.

"She'll be fine. Anyway, I can ask Mum to book Bob the farrier."

Mory was thrilled with Dancer's performance. Josh made them all line up, Midnight Dancer in the middle, while he took another photograph.

"I've finished the film. I'll send it off straight away."

"Great," said Mory. "Can I have a picture to go on my wall?"

"Sure."

"Well done, love," said Sheila. "I'm very impressed."

"I've been wanting to ride her for ages," said Mory.

"Patience pays," said David.

"Well, I did try once too soon, which was a mistake."

"Now she tells us."

The telephone rang. Sheila ran indoors to answer it. Mory turned Dancer out in the field with the others. A few minutes later Sheila emerged, looking flustered.

"It's Mr Jones. He says he's bringing the hens over this afternoon. I haven't got the run finished. He definitely told me next weekend."

At the bottom of the garden they viewed the new henhouse.

"It looks finished," said Mory.

"I like the laying boxes best," said Josh, lifting a lid. "Dead easy to get the eggs."

"Put Josh down for egg collection," said David.

"The wire netting needs nailing up," said Sheila. "Olwen says I'll have a fox in if the hens aren't thoroughly secured and I don't want them on the vegetable garden either."

"Noses to the grindstone," said David. "Where are you off to, Josh?"

"To take my camera indoors."

"I haven't heard that excuse before."

Josh grinned, "A good one, isn't it?" he said.

By lunchtime the netting was up and the outdoor run was ready.

"Now, if we can just run the netting along the bottom of the garden to the gate, they can have this wilderness to roam in too."

There was a general groan.

"Oh, all right. I suppose that's pushing my luck. Thanks for your help, everyone. That'll do for now. I must remember to borrow some chicken feed from Olwen."

"I'm starving. I'm going to get something to eat. Anyone else want something?" asked David. There was a chorus of yeses, so they gathered in the kitchen for some food.

It was gone two when Josh shouted that a van had arrived.

"Sheila, come and get your hens," called David.

The family spilled into the yard. Mory was surprised to see Lionel.

"Why aren't you at Penyworlod?" she asked.

"It's him. Won't let me," Lionel mumbled. Mory wanted to ask why but something about the look of Lionel's dad stopped her. He was an older version of Royden.

"I brought you eight to start," Mr Jones said. "They're at point of lay. Where do you want them?"

"At the bottom of the garden," Sheila said.

"Lionel!" His father's tone was sharp. Lionel started as though pinched. There were two crates in the back of the van. Lionel's dad pulled out one of them and the hens inside squawked. He held one end and Lionel struggled with the other. Sheila went to help.

"The boy can manage," said Mr Jones.

Lionel could, just about. He staggered down the garden path under his burden. David and Sheila quickly pulled out the other crate before Mr Jones could protest. Josh followed them.

"Fancy having a dad like that," said Mory. "He's horrid."

"It's odd Lionel isn't at Penyworlod," Cara said. "He always goes on Saturdays."

"His dad's stopped him."

"Why?"

"I don't know, do I?"

Back came Lionel, humping the empty crate. The girls helped him put it in the van.

"Why can't you go to Penyworlod?" Cara asked. Lionel nodded in the direction of his dad as if that said it all. He wouldn't talk about it.

Mory wanted to say come and look at Dancer but she didn't. She waited until Mr Jones and her parents brought back the other empty crate.

"Mum," Mory said. "Can Lionel stay to tea? We can take him home after, can't we?" Lionel looked surprised.

"Have you asked Lionel?" said Sheila.

"Can he, Mr Jones? We've got to get stones ready for school. We can do it together."

"Not today he can't," said Mr Jones. "He's got work to do."

"Tomorrow, then?"

"It depends."

"Can I ring in the morning? We'll come and fetch him, won't we, Mum?" Mory gave her mother a pleading look.

"Yes, of course we will," said Sheila. "He'd be most welcome."

All eyes turned to Mr Jones except Lionel's. There was a pause while Mr Jones considered.

"He can come on his bike," said Mr Jones. Lionel's mouth fell open. "Don't stand there gawping." Mr Jones gave Lionel a shove that nearly knocked him over. Lionel scrambled into the van. "If you want more hens, let me know."

"I will," said Sheila. "Thank you."

Mr Jones started the engine.

"Now what was that all about?" Sheila asked as the van drove out of the yard.

"I just thought it would be nice if Lionel came to tea, that's all," Mory said. "Can I make him a cake?"

"I don't see why not," said Sheila.

Cara offered to help and the two girls went into the kitchen. Mory rummaged in the fruit bowl and produced three bananas.

"How about a banana cake?" she said. "It's dead easy. The difficult bit is lining the bread tin with foil."

They busied themselves mashing bananas and weighing out raisins, nuts and flour. Mory fetched the margarine from the fridge and two eggs from the box on the window-sill.

"After you mash the bananas you just add everything and stir," she said. They were doing the stirring bit when Sheila came in and picked up the phone.

"You're getting flour all over the floor," she said as she dialled. Mory grimaced and carried on stirring. "Oh, hello, Olwen, it's Sheila."

"Baking powder," Mory said, suddenly remembering. She went to the cupboard. "Mum!"

"Be quiet. I'm talking. Yes, well the boy looked half-starved. I'd no idea he hadn't a mother. Is he all right, do you think?"

"Here it is," said Mory and spooned in a couple of teaspoonsful. Cara stirred until the baking powder disappeared.

"I hope Lionel likes it," she said, licking a finger. The mixture was ready.

"You haven't greased the tin," Sheila said and continued her conversation.

"Mothers do have their uses," said Mory, dropping a lump of margarine onto the foil and smearing it with her fingers. They poured the mixture into the tin and put the cake in the oven.

"And now the clearing up," Sheila said, putting the receiver down.

They piled the dirty things into the sink.

"I hate washing up," moaned Mory. "It's the worst bit." She handed Cara the mixing bowl to dry. "Why do you think Lionel's dad is so beastly to him?"

"Maybe he doesn't like Lionel very much," said Cara. Mory could well believe that.

"Mum," she said. "You and Dad like me and Josh, don't you?"

"Most of the time," Sheila said. Mory looked pensive. "Of course we like you." Sheila put her arms round her daughter. "What's more, we love you to bits. What brought this on?"

"Nothing," Mory said. "I'm glad I'm not Lionel." Sheila gave her an understanding squeeze.

"Yes, I know what you mean."

The next afternoon at three o'clock, a bicycle rattled into the yard. Lionel came to a stop and leaned his bike against the wall. Mory went to greet him.

"Hello," she said. Lionel was hot from his ride. "How far is it?"

"About four miles," he said. "Uphill till the last bit."

"Do you want a drink?"

"It's all right," said Lionel.

"The others are up at Llangabby riding. They'll be back soon. We made a banana cake."

"Banana cake! Sounds weird," said Lionel.

"Wait till you taste it." They stood awkwardly for a moment. "Do you want to see Dancer?" Lionel nodded. Mory led the way to the field gate and called. The pony lifted her head.

"She's nice," said Lionel.

"She's all black except for a tuft of white at the bottom of her mane," said Mory.

Dancer came over and nuzzled for something to eat. Lionel put his hand in his pocket and slowly took it out again, empty.

"Here," said Mory. "I've got loads." Lionel helped himself to some pony nuts and Dancer gobbled them.

"You ridden her?"

"I've just started. I rode round the field on my own this morning."

Lionel sniffed Dancer's nose and Dancer sniffed his.

"Making friends?"

"Horse language," said Lionel. "It's hello."

There was a clatter of hooves in the yard.

"Here are the others," said Mory. Dancer whinnied.

Mory and Lionel helped untack Misty and Rustler. Then the four of them went in the kitchen. A wonderful smell of cooking greeted them.

"I've made some jam tarts to go with the cake," said Sheila. "They'll be ready in a few minutes. Show Lionel where the loo is."

Lionel tucked into the cake and the jam tarts with a vengeance. Mory wondered if he'd been saving up all day. Josh grinned.

"What's the matter?" Lionel asked.

"You've got jam on your nose," said Josh. Lionel's cheeks glowed pink. He wiped his nose on his sleeve, ignoring the kitchen roll Mory offered.

"Shall we go and look for stones?" Mory asked.

"Dad's had some chippings delivered," said Cara. "There's some lovely white stone in with the granite."

"Let's go to Llangabby then."

They walked up and Lionel pushed his bike.

"Why won't your dad let you go to Penyworlod any more?" Mory asked.

"He don't want me working for nothing."

"But you get riding lessons."

"He wants money. What I say don't count. That's it."

They arrived at the top of the track and were about to turn into the Llangabby yard when a motorbike roared up the lane. Instinctively, Lionel looked for somewhere to hide. He was too late. The bike skidded to a halt. It was Royden. Lionel paled under his freckles.

"What are you doing here, brat?" Royden said, his voice muffled under the helmet.

"He's been to tea with us," said Mory.

Royden pulled his helmet off.

"He can answer. He's a big boy now."

"It's what she said. Dad let me."

"Oh, did he? Well you just let on one word to him that you've seen me and I'll have you. Got it?" Royden pulled his helmet back on and roared off.

"What's in that box?" Josh asked.

"Don't know," said Lionel. He looked scared.

They made for the pile of chippings. While the others rummaged, looking for unusual stones, Lionel chose one quickly and said, "I'm going. All right if I take this one?"

"Fine," said Cara.

"Thanks for tea. See you." He put the stone in his pocket, grabbed his bike and was gone.

"That's rotten," said Mory. "He was enjoying himself until Royden came."

SEVEN

Precious Stones

At school the following morning, there was a stirring of interest in the junior class. Everyone had brought stones. Mory's, a piece of granite with white quartz flecks and Cara's, a lump of pink and white quartz, were from the chippings pile. In the end, Josh brought his special flint found on the chalk downs near Waring. The flint was heavy but not as heavy as Gareth's stone, which was huge.

"It's from the rockery," Gareth said. "I've got to put it back."

Lionel placed his stone in front of him, a small piece of white quartz, and wrapped a hand around it. Sarah's was a lucky stone, one with a hole in the middle.

"If I want a wish I spit through it and chuck it over my shoulder," she said. "What did you bring, Caroline?"

"A diamond."

The news buzzed round the class and caused a sensation.

"That's not a stone," said Gareth.

"Yes, it is," said Caroline. "It came out of the ground, didn't it?" That shut Gareth up.

"I bet it's not a real one," Sarah said.

"Of course it's a real one. Mummy wouldn't have a fake."

It took until the afternoon to get to stones. Everyone wanted to see Caroline's diamond. At lunchtime any request was met with a stubborn refusal. In the afternoon there was almost a cheer when Mrs Wynne said it was time to start on the project.

"This is something the whole class can do together," she said. "It's going to be about the earth. About how the earth began and formed its rocks and minerals. Now, have you all brought your stones?"

There were lots of loud yeses and one tiny no. Ian Evans had left his on his doorstep.

"Bring it tomorrow, Ian."

"Yes, Miss," said Ian.

Mrs Wynne went round the class and one at a time they held up their stone and said where it had come from. Gareth had a struggle to lift his and this caused some hilarity. When it was Caroline's turn everyone waited with baited breath.

"Caroline, did you bring a stone?" Mrs Wynne asked.

"It's here." Caroline rummaged in her pocket and

took out a small black box. She opened the lid. Children stood up, trying to see.

"Sit down, everyone," said Mrs Wynne. "Bring it to me please, Caroline, and tell me what it is." Mrs Wynne must have been the only person not to know.

"It's a diamond."

"A diamond! Your diamond?"

"No, it's Mummy's," said Caroline.

"I hope your mother knows you've brought it."

"Oh, yes. It's not her best one. It's set in a ring."

"So it is." Mrs Wynne took out the ring. "Take it round to each table and give everyone a chance to see it."

Caroline, full of self-importance, enjoyed herself immensely. She said the diamond had come from a mine in Africa and that it hadn't glittered as it did now until it was cut and polished in Holland.

"Showing off again," said Mory.

When everyone had seen the diamond, Caroline sat down and closed the box. Mrs Wynne told them a little more about diamonds. They were much sought after, she said, and, as they were very hard, were used for cutting things like glass. They were so valuable that people risked their lives to find them deep in the earth.

"What do we call a stone like a diamond? Yes, Sarah."

"A hard stone."

"Yes, but I'm looking for a particular word. Yes Josh."

"A precious stone."

"Yes, it's a precious stone. What other sorts of precious stones are there?"

Mrs Wynne went round the class collecting names. Rubies, emeralds, sapphires, amethysts, garnets. Then Mrs Wynne asked what colour each of the stones were. When she got to sapphires she asked Josh.

"Blue," said Josh.

"Has anyone seen a sapphire?"

Only Mory, Josh, Cara and Caroline put up their hands.

"Mum's got a sapphire necklace," said Josh. "It belonged to our great-grandmother."

"I bet it's not real," whispered Caroline. "Sapphires are valuable."

"Of course it's real," said Mory. Caroline pulled an I-don't-believe you face.

"Better bring it and show me," she said. "It's easy to spot a fake. I bet yours is."

"Oh, yes, and you'd know of course."

"Yes, Mummy has a sapphire brooch."

"That's enough whispering, Mory and Caroline," said Mrs Wynne and went on to amethysts.

Mory couldn't concentrate after that. She was furious. Very well, if Caroline was such an expert she would bring the necklace and show her. She'd bring it tomorrow. Then Caroline would see it was real sapphires.

All the way home Mory wrestled with herself. Should she ask her mother or should she "borrow" the necklace without asking, in case Sheila said no? In the end she decided to borrow it. It was a relief to decide. After eating, she rode Dancer round the field and watched television with Josh. Then a little time before bed she checked to see where her parents were – outside in the pottery. Leaving Josh in front of the television, she went upstairs.

Creeping along the landing, Mory refused to listen to the little voice that told her she shouldn't be doing this. Losing face with Caroline Spencer was more than she could bear. She opened her parents' bedroom door and went in, taking the jewellery case from the second drawer of the dressing table. Mory opened the lid. The sapphires sparkled. With shaking fingers she removed the necklace, put the case away and hurried out.

Scuttling into her own room, with thumping heart, she wrapped the necklace in several tissues and zipped it safely inside her belt bag. Putting the bag under her pillow she breathed a sigh of relief. Tomorrow she would wear the bag all day. The necklace would be quite safe.

Feeling shaky, Mory went outside. It was getting dark and a light was on in the pottery. She poked her head round the door and found her mother

poring over a wiring diagram and her father screwing up a shelf bracket. They looked up when they heard the door. For one awful moment Mory thought they knew.

"It's time for bed," said Sheila. Guilt turned Mory bright pink.

"I'm going to say good night to the ponies first," she said, hurrying away, feeling like a thief. She had a strong urge to put the necklace back but it didn't last. Caroline Spencer was not going to call her a liar and get away with it.

In bed Mory tossed and turned. It was too much for Splodge. He jumped from the bed and curled up on a sweater. Once Mory woke in a panic, dreaming she had lost the necklace. She felt for the belt bag. It was still there, safe under her pillow. It was not too late to change her mind but she knew she wouldn't.

In the morning Mory put the belt bag in her school bag. She would wear it as soon as they left the house. She hardly ate any breakfast.

"Mory, are you feeling all right?" Sheila asked.

"I'm fine," Mory said. "I don't feel hungry, that's all." Luckily for her, the phone rang. It was for Sheila. David handed over the receiver.

"Might be a job. It's the headteacher from Aberdawl Comprehensive."

Mory and Josh pulled on their anoraks.

"Better get going, you two," said David.

As soon as they were out of the yard, Mory fastened the belt bag round her waist.

"What have you got in there?" Josh asked.

"Some tissues. I think I might be getting a cold." Mory blushed at the lie and walked ahead.

They joined Cara at the top of the track and the three of them made their way down the lane for the bus. They were nearly at the bottom when Sheila, tooting behind, wound down the window.

"I'm going into Aberdawl to do some supply teaching," she called. "Do you want a lift?"

"Don't worry about us," said Mory. "We'll get the bus."

Sheila left them to wait and, shortly after, the bus arrived. They clambered aboard and joined the others at the back. Mory felt better once they were on the move but really she wished the day was over and the necklace safely back in the drawer.

Caroline arrived when Mory was hanging up her anorak.

"I don't suppose you've brought it?" she said.

"Of course I have," said Mory.

"Then show me."

"Not now," said Mory. Cara overheard and hurried after her.

"Mory, have you brought Aunt Sheila's necklace?"

"She called me a liar. I'm proving her wrong."

"But Mory. . ."

They sat down. Caroline wouldn't let the subject drop. "Show me now."

"Will you shut up," said Mory. "I don't want everyone to know."

"Frightened I'll say it's a fake," smirked Caroline.

"It's not a fake." It was too late for secrecy now. Everyone at their table was listening. "All right," said Mory and unzipped her belt bag. She took out the necklace and unwrapped it from its cocoon of tissues. The pale blue sapphires sparkled. Sarah gasped in admiration.

"It's beautiful," she said. "It doesn't look like a fake." Lionel leaned over and touched it.

"Phew!" Gareth whistled. "I bet that's worth a lot."

"If it's genuine," said Caroline.

"I thought you said you could tell," said Mory.

"Some fakes need an expert to tell."

"At least you admit you're not that," snapped

Mory. A crowd had gathered round the table and Josh joined it.

"Does Mum know?" he whispered. Mory didn't reply. He looked at Cara. She shrugged. Mrs Wynne and Mrs Pugh came in. Quickly Mory wrapped the necklace in its tissues and stuffed it back in her bag.

Soon everyone in the class knew Mory had brought the necklace. It had been a stupid mistake.

"The trouble with you," she whispered to Caroline, "is that you wouldn't know a genuine sapphire from a peanut."

"We'll let Mrs Wynne decide, shall we?" said Caroline and put up her hand. Mory was overcome with rage. She kicked Caroline under the table. Caroline let out a yowl of pain which brought Mrs Wynne across the room in no time.

"What's going on?" she asked.

"She kicked me," said Caroline, rubbing her leg. Mrs Wynne looked at Mory's furious face.

"It's my experience that people don't usually kick other people without provocation," she said. "I want to know what's going on. We'll go outside and discuss it now. Both of you."

Caroline and Mory followed Mrs Wynne from the classroom. It was a relief for Mory to tell the truth, even though she knew she was in for trouble. Caroline smirked self-righteously.

"Where is the necklace?" Mrs Wynne asked.

Mory handed it to Mrs Wynne.

"Mory, you do realise that you have taken an enormous risk?" Mory nodded. I think I'd better look after it. I shall take both you and it home after school." Mory blushed with shame. "All right, Mory, you can go." Mory walked towards the classroom.

"I don't think you have anything to be proud of in all this, Caroline," was the last thing she heard before she went in. It didn't make her feel any better.

At lunchtime, both Josh and Cara told her she was an idiot. Although she wouldn't agree she knew they were right.

"Do you think Mrs Wynne's going to tell Mum?" Josh said.

"I don't know," said Mory.

The rest of the class wanted Mrs Wynne to show them the sapphire necklace but she never even mentioned it. At the end of the day, Cara and Josh waited in the playground with Mory.

"Can they come too?" Mory asked, when Mrs Wynne was ready to go.

"Yes, they can," she said. The three of them followed Mrs Wynne to the gate.

They were startled by an agonised yell. In the road Royden had hold of Lionel by the hair and was twisting his ear. Mory tensed with anger. Royden let go when he saw Mrs Wynne.

"Once a bully always a bully it seems, Royden. I will not have that kind of behaviour outside my school."

"Who's going to stop me?" Royden sneered. "You and whose army?"

Mrs Wynne's face took on a certain look. But before she could say anything, Mory charged.

"You pig!" she shouted, punching and kicking. "You horrid pig."

"That's enough, Mory!" shouted Mrs Wynne, pulling Mory out of reach as Royden lashed out.

"Leave Lionel alone, can't you?" Mory raged. "Pick on someone your own size."

With eyes fixed on his attacker, Royden wiped his lip.

"I'll get you for this," he said. Pulling on his helmet, he started his motorbike. He rode off before anything else was said.

"Whatever got into you, Mory?" Mrs Wynne said. Mory trembled. "What a silly thing to do."

As if coming out of a daze, Lionel jumped on his bicycle and pedalled off.

"No more behaviour like this, Mory. Losing your temper serves no purpose at all. With Royden it makes matters worse. Do you understand?" Mory nodded. "Let's get you home."

"I'm sorry," said Mory. "It's just that. . ." Mrs Wynne put a hand on her shoulder.

"I know," she said.

EIGHT

Chased

Mory sat in the front of the car next to Mrs Wynne, the others in the back. It was a silent journey. Mrs Wynne was deep in thought and the three youngsters were too shaken to talk. They drove past Royden, sitting astride his motorbike in a layby. He swung out and followed them.

"Don't worry, Mory," said Mrs Wynne. "I'm taking you all the way home." Mory's heart sank. It looked as if her parents were going to find out after all. She looked over her shoulder. Royden was right behind them. They turned into the lane and stopped outside Llangabby Farm.

"Do you want to get out here, Cara?" Mrs Wynne asked.

"Thank you," said Cara. Royden drove past.

"How do I get you to Black Rock Farm?" Mrs Wynne asked when Cara had closed the door.

"Turn left there," said Mory, pointing. "Down the track. But there's no need to drive us. We can walk."

"I'm taking you. I want to see you safely home and I'd like a word with your parents." Mory bit her lip. It was as she had thought. If it hadn't been for Caroline she wouldn't be in this mess. Mrs Wynne leaned over and opened her briefcase. She took out the necklace.

"I shan't tell your parents that you took this if you promise to put it straight back where it belongs and not to do anything like it again."

"I promise," said Mory. "I won't. Really, I won't." Mrs Wynne gave Mory the necklace.

"So whether you tell them or not is up to you."

"Yes, thank you, Mrs Wynne." Mory was really grateful.

Mrs Wynne drove onto the track and the car bounced down to Black Rock.

"Turn in here," said Mory, pointing to the yard entrance. Mrs Wynne drove in and switched off the engine.

"Now, go and put that necklace away," she said. "Ah, here's your father." Mory didn't need telling twice, especially when she saw David's look of concern.

"Is anything wrong?" he asked.

"Nothing serious," said Mrs Wynne, getting out of the car. "I wonder if I can have a word?"

"Of course. Would you like some tea?"

"No thanks, but you can show me your pottery if you like."

"I'd be delighted."

It didn't look as if Sheila was back yet. Mory scooted across the yard and was in the house and up the stairs as fast as her legs would take her. She flung open her parents' bedroom door. She put the necklace in the jewellery case and closed the drawer. She collapsed on the bed with a sigh of relief.

Josh joined her.

"If she's not telling about the necklace, what is she telling?" he asked.

"I don't know," said Mory.

The two of them sat in silence until feet on the stairs startled them. Guiltily, they went onto the landing to be met by Sheila.

"David's making tea. Go and help him, Josh. Chop, chop." Josh took the hint and scurried downstairs.

"We've got to have a little talk," Sheila said, leading the way to Mory's room.

With sinking heart, Mory followed. Had Mrs Wynne changed her mind and told about the necklace after all?

"Sit down," said Sheila. "It was kind of Mrs Wynne to bring you home." Mory didn't reply. She was on tenterhooks, wondering what was coming next. "She told us about the rivalry between you and Caroline Spencer which she feels might get you into trouble if it's taken too far." Mory sighed. "I do understand that Caroline aggravates you but you must try not to let it get to you." Mory nodded.

"I will try," she said. "I have tried. But she goes on and on about how rotten Dancer is and makes digs about us being poor."

"Why, do you think?"

"I don't know." Then Mory remembered what Cara had said. "Cara thinks she's jealous because I'm making a success of Dancer."

"What do you think?"

"Could be. I just wish she'd lay off."

"I think Cara has a point. And feeling cross with you for being successful where she failed can't be very nice for her or you."

"No," said Mory.

"Shall I tell you what I think?"

"What?"

"I think Caroline's lonely. She's desperate for attention and tries to get it by showing off. Inside she feels very small and unappreciated. Your success with Dancer has made her feel even smaller."

"But she gets everything she wants. You should see her riding gear."

"It's things like riding gear she criticises you for. But there are things you do have which probably Caroline has never had." Mory was beginning to see where this was leading.

"You mean like being able to leave our stuff all over the house."

"That's part of it, isn't it? It shows you belong

here. That Dad and I love and accept you. You and your bits and bobs. They're a part of you, aren't they? Although, goodness knows, I long for a tidy house," said Sheila, laughing.

"Do you mean she doesn't get hugs?"

"I don't know. I'm sure her parents love her as much as they can. But I don't think they find children easy to understand. They'd be surprised to think her lonely, for instance. They provide lots of things but things aren't enough, are they? Talking to one another and being understood is important too."

"Like we are now, you mean?"

"Exactly like that."

Mory thought for a few moments with her chin on her hands.

"I'll try not to let her get to me and I'll try and be nicer but it's really hard."

"Look before you leap, my love. If you could only do that I'm sure it would help. Which leads me to something very serious," said Sheila. "Your attack on Royden Jones."

"But he twisted Lionel's ear and pulled his hair."

"Mrs Wynne was quite capable of dealing with the situation. Losing your temper may have made you a dangerous enemy. Apparently Royden is, to put it bluntly, a bully."

"I know," said Mory. "I'll keep out of his way."

"Make sure you do, and please, please, try and

control that temper. I don't want you getting hurt."
Sheila gave Mory's hand a squeeze. "None of us do."

They went downstairs to the kitchen where
David was boiling the kettle. Mrs Wynne had gone.
He made a pot of tea and put it on the table. Sheila
collected some mugs.

"Who wants tea?" Josh wanted juice and fetched
some from the fridge.

"Bring some milk as well," said David.

"Let's finish off the banana cake," said Sheila,
"to celebrate my first day's teaching in Wales." Mory
took out the cake tin.

"What's the school like?" David asked.

"It seems all right. A nice friendly staff. I enjoyed my day."

There was a knock at the door. It was Cara.

"Anyone going riding?" she asked.

"Certainly am," said Mory, stuffing in her last piece of banana cake. "Want a bit?"

"Mory, at least finish your mouthful," said David.

"I've had tea, thanks," said Cara. "Let's take Dancer up through the fields."

"Great idea," said Mory.

"Be careful," said Sheila.

"Mum," said Mory. "Don't worry."

Once outside, Cara wanted to know what happened with Mrs Wynne. Mory told her.

"She's great, isn't she? It was really nice of her not to tell about the necklace."

"Yes, but she did tell about me and Caroline and me punching Royden. Now Mum wants me to be nice to Caroline and she's worried Royden's going to bash me up."

"He might try," said Cara.

"Do you think so? Well, I'll be careful."

Mory was too excited about the ride to worry about Royden. The ponies were soon ready and they set off, Misty leading the way, followed by Dancer, followed by Rustler. They thought Dancer would feel safest in the middle. As it was they needn't have worried, she was quite happy. Going out was nothing new to her. It was being ridden that was new and she was getting used to that.

They walked down the track and at the gate near the bottom, Cara jumped off, giving Misty's reins to Josh. The gate catch had rusted but at last she got it open. She led Misty through and the others followed. Cara closed the gate behind them and mounted. They turned the ponies towards Llangabby. The field sloped down for a while and then began to climb.

"Shall we trot?" Cara asked.

"Yes, let's," said Mory. Dancer trotted obediently to the next gate.

"Walk," said Mory. Dancer walked and Mory patted her. "Good girl."

"I'll do this one," said Josh, jumping off. He'd opened this gate lots of times for Uncle Glyn.

"Let's canter to the next gate," said Mory.

"Are you sure?" asked Cara.

"We've got to canter sometime."

"Make it a nice slow one, then," said Cara.

They set off. Mory kept Dancer behind Misty. She didn't want her to race and she did want her to stop, so this seemed a good idea. Rustler set off at quite a lick and Dancer, enjoying cantering with her friends, put in a whopping buck. Mory, quite unprepared, went flying and hit the ground with a thud.

"Oh, no," groaned Cara, turning Misty. She rode back to where Mory was slowly getting up.

"Are you all right?" she asked.

"Yes," said Mory, rubbing her arm and feeling a dismal failure.

"Well, that's something you've found out. When she's excited she's going to buck. You've got to sit back to it and keep her head up."

"Yes."

"Do you want to try again?"

"Of course," said Mory.

Josh, grinning, led Dancer back to her. The pony seemed surprised to have lost her rider.

"She didn't know you'd fall off when she bucked," Josh said. "She promises not to do it again."

"Ha, ha," said Mory but to her relief, Dancer didn't do it again. They took the ponies back to the bottom of the field and cantered up it once more.

They were halfway up when an engine roared into life. The top gate swung open and a red motorbike tore down the field towards them.

"Split up," yelled Cara, turning Misty. Josh turned Rustler the other way. Dancer followed him. The motorcyclist steered towards the two ponies. Mory turned Dancer down the field away from Rustler. Dancer came to a stop, wanting to follow her friend, then, realising the bike was coming towards her, began leaping sideways. Somehow Mory managed to stay on.

The bike circled the pony and when her opportunity came, Mory urged Dancer back up the field. The pony shot forward. Out of the corner of her eye, Mory caught sight of a black and white dog streaking down the field. It was Mab, Uncle Glyn's border collie. Dancer joined the others at the top of the field and slowed.

"Whoa," Mory told her. "Whoa." She stroked the pony's neck while she jogged to a standstill and watched the dog circle the motorbike as if it was a sheep.

A whistle from the gate sent Mab in. She ran in front of the bike, causing it to swerve. Mab snapped at Royden's legs. Another whistle and she broke away, lying down until the bike started down the field, when she crossed its path again. The children and the ponies watched, fascinated.

Slowly, the dog forced the bike up the field and back to the gate, keeping it on the move by snapping at the rider if he stopped. As the bike arrived at the gate it closed and Uncle Glyn stood before the rider, leaning on his stick.

The children stayed where they were, so they didn't hear what was said. At last Uncle Glyn opened the gate and the motorbike roared off. The children rode over to him.

"Are you all right?" Uncle Glyn asked.

They were. Remarkably, none of the ponies seemed frightened, even the inexperienced Dancer. On the contrary, they seemed to have enjoyed their mad gallop.

"Royden Jones! I've told him that if I ever see him on my land again, I'll destroy his bike first and fetch the police after," said Uncle Glyn. "He's got a nerve. I've had my eye on him. Backwards and forwards into the hills. I've warned him and he knows I mean it. You'd better take the ponies back quietly by the track."

"Thank you, Mab," said Josh. Mab looked up, her pink tongue lolling from the corner of her mouth. Josh felt she was smiling.

They rode in silence. Out through the top field,

across the yard at Llangabby and onto the track. It was Mory who spoke first.

"That was lucky," she said. "Thank goodness for Mab."

"I don't think he'll come back after that," said Cara. "Royden was lucky Dad didn't send for the police."

"Hell's bells," said Mory. "What's Mum going to say?"

"How did you get on?" was Sheila's first question when they got back.

"Dancer was fantastic, apart from when she bucked."

"And what happened to you?"

"I fell off."

"And lived, I see," said David.

"Oh, Mory," said Sheila. "Sometimes I wish you had a properly trained pony."

"She is properly trained and she's getting more properly trained every day. The worst thing was when Royden chased us on his motorbike."

"But Uncle Glyn and Mab sorted him out," said Josh.

"So everything's all right," said Mory, more brightly than she felt.

"No, everything's not all right," said Sheila and Mory knew she was right. It wasn't.

NINE

Hiding Places

At school the next day Mory was walking across the playground when Lionel came up to her. He was pale and drawn, with a horribly swollen ear.

"Are you all right?" she asked.

"I got something to tell you," Lionel said. He looked over his shoulder and drew close. "Promise not to tell anyone."

"All right," said Mory, wondering what was coming next.

"Say it."

"I promise."

"Royden knows about the sapphire necklace."

"What does that matter?" Mory asked. Lionel looked uncomfortable. A memory shimmered in Mory's head, Mrs Pugh at the shop hearing a motorbike the night they were robbed. She stared at Lionel's disturbed face, a realisation slowly dawning. "You mean Royden robbed the shop . . ."

Lionel nodded.

". . .and took the school fund money?"

"I told him where it was. He was mad it was so little. Clouted me for that. He makes me spy. I don't want to. I didn't mean to say about the necklace, only . . ."

"That's terrible."

"Don't tell."

"But I should go to the police."

"Where's the proof? Where's the nicked stuff? I don't know. Royden'd say I was lying. He'd kill me. And what about me spying?" Mory could see the danger. It put her in a quandary. She had promised. Lionel had only told because of that promise.

"He's out to get that necklace. Because you bashed him and because he thinks it's easy. He's cocky, see. You stop him."

"Hell's bells, Lionel," said Mory. "How?" Her mind raced. "Look, can I tell Josh and Cara? I'll need help."

"If they promise. Don't drop me in it."

"I won't," said Mory. "I'll tell them after school."

Mory spent the rest of the day in a daze, longing to get home, longing to be able to do something. She didn't notice Caroline, she didn't notice anything particularly. Her mind focused on the necklace and nothing else.

At last they were on their way home and the moment they got off the bus Mory swore Josh and Cara to secrecy.

"Royden is the thief," she said, and told them the rest.

"But Mory," said Cara. "We must tell the police."

"We can't, we simply can't. Think what might happen to Lionel. Home for a council of war. But first I'm going to get the necklace, if it's still there."

Mory raced ahead, leaving the others to digest the startling news. She pelted along the lane and down the track. Pausing by the yard entrance to regain her breath, she crept across, wanting to get indoors without David seeing. She managed without difficulty. How easy it would be for Royden to do the same. The house was empty. She ran upstairs to her parents' bedroom, took out the jewellery case and opened the lid. What a relief to see the sapphires sparkle.

"I must find a hiding place," she said. "But where?" She couldn't think of anywhere indoors. "The hayloft! No thief would think of looking for jewellery in a barn."

She fastened the lid and closed the drawer. Running to her own room, she put the jewellery case in a plastic bag and quickly changed out of her school things. She bumped into Josh on the landing.

"Quick," she said. "I'm going to hide the jewellery case in the hayloft."

"You can't," said Josh. "When Mum opens the

drawer, she'll see the case is missing. Just take the necklace. It can go in my wooden box."

"Brains, Josh. Why didn't I think of that?"

They put the sapphire necklace into Josh's box and put the empty case back in the drawer.

"Mum never wears the necklace unless she's going somewhere," said Josh.

"You're right. We can bring it in as soon as she needs it," said Mory. "The perfect solution."

It was gloomy in the barn and there was no light, so they had to feel their way to the hayloft steps. Mory tripped and banged her knee.

"Ouch," she said.

"You all right?"

"Watch the bottom step," she said. "It's not where you think it is."

They arrived in the hayloft without further mishap and, as their eyes adjusted to the gloom, they were able to see more clearly. At first they were disappointed. There didn't seem to be any likely hiding places. There was nothing underneath the floorboards but a drop to the ground. There were no nooks or crannies.

"What about in the rafters?" said Josh.

Mory peered at the old, uneven beams criss-crossing above them.

"There might be a space somewhere," said Josh. "Let's bring the ladder up and look."

"It's worth a try, I suppose."

They heaved the ladder up the steps. It was tricky because of the corner. Josh insisted on carrying it to the far end of the barn, where they leaned it against the wall.

"I'll go up," said Josh.

"Hang on. I'll hold it."

Mory steadied the ladder and Josh climbed up.

"The box could go on this beam," he said.

"No," said Mory. "You'd see it from here."

"Wait a minute," said Josh. "There's a space where the beam goes into the wall. One of the stones is loose."

"Can you get it out?"

"Yes, I think so."

Lumps of crumbling mortar pattered to the floor.

"Watch out," said Mory.

"Sorry."

Josh freed the stone.

"It'll be just our luck if the whole roof collapses," said Mory.

"Not a chance," said Josh. "I'm coming down."

"I'll take the box up," said Mory. "Then I can see what it's like. Hold the ladder."

Mory picked up the carrier bag and climbed up. It was as Josh had said, a secret space. Pushing against the ladder with her knees, she freed both hands and was able to wrap the bag around the box and push it into the hole. Then lifting the stone from the rafter, she wedged it in place.

"How's that?" she asked.

"You'd never think of looking there in a million years," said Josh. "Wait till you come down and you'll see what I mean."

Josh was right. Only the fallen mortar gave a clue to the hiding place.

"Better sweep the floor," said Mory.

"I'll get the brush," said Josh, heading for the stairs. "There's something I want from indoors." Mory pulled the ladder across the loft ready to take down.

On his way back, Josh met Cara in the yard.

"Where've you been?" she asked. "I've been looking for you everywhere."

"Finding a hiding place for the you know what," said Josh, grabbing the broom. "Come up to the hayloft and guess where it is."

Cara searched while Mory brushed the floor.

"I don't know," she said.

"A clue," said Josh. "It's up not down."

Cara looked at the beams from all angles.

"I give up," she said. "Where is it?"

"Up there," said Mory, pointing.

"There's a secret hole," said Josh. "And you need the ladder to get to it."

"How did you find it?"

"Followed my nose," said Josh.

"Let's get out of here," said Mory. The air was murky with dust and her throat felt dry.

It was easier taking the ladder down with three of them.

"One last thing," said Josh, taking a reel of brown cotton from his pocket. He tied the cotton so it stretched as an invisible barrier across the bottom of the stairs.

"If it's broken, we'll know someone's been up here."

"Brilliant, Josh," said Mory. "How did you think of that?"

"Read it in a book."

They held their council of war in one of the stables. Mory, having pondered all day about what to do, had come to the conclusion that they must find Royden's hiding place.

"What good will that do," said Cara, "now we've promised not to tell on him?"

"I don't know," said Mory. "But at least we'll know where he is."

"And where the stolen stuff is," said Cara.

"Yes," said Josh. "He'll think he's safe when he's not."

"If he's still there," said Cara.

"Do you think he's gone?" Mory asked.

"He might have, with Dad threatening to tell the police."

"Well, let's find out."

They brought the ponies in and got them ready. Dancer was delighted to be coming in with the others.

"She doesn't want to miss the fun," said Josh.

"If it's going to be fun," said Mory. She had to admit she felt scared. Her fear grew less as soon as she was on Dancer. A pony was much more sure-footed on the hills than a motorbike. They shouted goodbye and David came out of the pottery to wave them off on what he thought was an ordinary ride.

"Be careful," he said to Mory.

"I will," she replied.

They turned onto the track. The plan was to follow the route Mory had taken on Rustler. They rode in the same order as the previous day, Misty in front, Dancer next and Rustler behind. When they came onto the ridge they looked for signs of Royden. Moorland stretched all round them and the only living things to be seen were sheep in the heather dotted here and there and a far-off bird in the sky.

"Better get a move on," said Cara. "We don't want to run out of time."

Misty set the pace and they were soon cantering along the edge of the track. Dancer was full of go and Mory made sure to keep the pony's head up in case she tried another buck. At the top of the hill they reached the place where Mory had turned back. Here Misty slowed. Dancer reined in easily. It was Rustler who pulled to go on but Josh was firm. They followed the motorbike tracks onto the small path.

"This way leads over the next hill and into the forest," said Cara.

"Forest!" said Josh. "I didn't know there was a forest."

"Yes, the Forestry Commission owns acres of land that way. It stretches for miles. It's a bit far from us unless you're going to ride all day. I've only been once on a pony club trek."

They followed the path down and up again and it was quite stony. The ponies picked their way carefully.

"Must be bumpy on a bike," said Josh.

Suddenly there was a panorama of pine trees stretching into the distance. Down they went until they came to a gate that led into a forestry enclosure. It had a rusty old padlock and chain around it.

"It's locked," said Mory.

"It can't be," said Cara. "The bike tracks lead here."

Mory dismounted and handed her reins to Cara.

"You're right," she said, looking more carefully. "It's a trick. The chain hooks over a nail at the back." She unhooked the chain and opened the gate. After the ponies had gone through, she closed it, leaving the chain hooked as before.

Before them was a hard forestry road of stone chippings.

"Try and keep off the stones, Mory," said Cara. "They'll damage Dancer's feet. She really needs shoes for this."

"It's impossible to be sure of the bike tracks now," said Josh.

As if on cue, an engine roared angrily to life, threatening them from somewhere in the forest. They looked at one another, alarmed.

"Hide," said Mory. Quickly they led the ponies into the trees, stopping far enough from the road not to be seen.

"Stay here. I'm going to see if it's Royden," said Mory.

She moved from tree to tree until she had a good view of the road. The engine drew closer and a red motorbike raced into view. It *was* Royden. There was no mistaking the big box on the back. Now Mory had an idea of what was inside – burglar's tools!

Royden stopped and opened the gate. Mory had a sudden panic. Had they left hoof prints? If there were any, Royden didn't seem to see them. He drove through the gate, closed it and set off up the track. When he was out of sight, Mory ran back to the others.

"It was him. He's gone. The going's clear ahead."

"He can't have come from far," said Josh as they led the ponies back to the road. "He was here quite quickly from the time we heard the engine start."

"I'll lead Dancer," said Mory, "to save her feet."

Running water could be heard to their right where the land fell into a valley but they couldn't see the stream for trees and undergrowth. Rounding the bend ahead, they came to a place where several large beech trees grew at the foot of a rock face and a path went down towards the water.

"Look," said Mory. "Motorbike tracks."

"I don't think we should take the ponies in case Royden comes back," said Cara. "And they'll leave hoofprints."

"Stay with them, Josh," said Mory.

"Why me?"

"It's all right, I'll stay," said Cara. "Help me lead the ponies into the trees out of sight. I'll be fine under cover."

Once Cara and the ponies were safe, Mory and Josh set off down the path. It was steep, more rock than earth. Easy to ride up or down on a motorbike whatever the weather.

They arrived in a clearing where sheer rock towered above them and water tumbled loudly nearby.

"A waterfall," said Mory loud enough for Josh to hear. He nodded.

Walking towards the water, they saw a shed, almost hidden, behind some brambles. It was green with lichen and must have been there for a long time. The door was padlocked. Mory and Josh looked knowingly at one another. The shed was old but the padlock was new.

Mory put her finger to her lips. She walked round the shed, found a window and peered in. The glass was dirty and inside was dark. She could just make out a tea chest with a mug on it and a sleeping bag on the floor. Mory wondered what else was locked in there.

Josh pulled her sleeve. Turning, Mory saw the remains of a recent fire. But it wasn't the fire Josh was pointing to. Under a curtain of ivy which grew down the rockface was a low, dark hole.

They crept towards it. With her back to the rock, Mory signed for Josh to stay where he was and scrambled under the ivy. She entered a cave, pitch black and cold. Shivering, she stretched up to find the roof. It must have been high, she couldn't reach it. She edged forward. One, two, three, four, five paces. On the sixth she stumbled against a wall. She looked about, her eyes beginning to focus in the dim light. A stack of wood by the entrance was all she could make out, put there, no doubt, to keep dry. To see properly she needed a torch. She crawled outside.

"It's a big cave," she said, voice raised against the falling water. "I couldn't see very well. I should think he keeps most of his stuff locked in the shed."

"Shall we check out the waterfall?" Josh said. Mory shook her head.

"Better go in case he comes back. We've no way of hearing with all this noise."

They were at the top of the path when they heard the motorbike. Startled, they pelted across the road and into the trees. Recovering, they moved cautiously to where Cara and the ponies were waiting.

"Just in time," Mory said, her heart thumping against her chest.

The ponies pricked their ears, and they and their riders kept very still as Royden slowed his motorbike and turned down the path to the clearing. Suspended from the box on the carrier were two dead rabbits.

"He's been hunting," said Mory.

"What with?" said Josh. "He hasn't got a gun."

"Snares, I bet," said Cara. "Trust him."

"I think we should get out of here," said Mory, "in case he comes back. He won't hear us. The water's incredibly noisy down there."

At the edge of the trees Josh and Cara mounted. Looking and listening anxiously, they walked to the gate, Mory leading Dancer. Safely through and the gate chained up, Mory mounted. Looking back, she saw a thin column of smoke drift above the trees. Royden cooking his rabbits, she thought.

"Come on, Mory," said Josh.

"I am," she said and they set off, at a fast trot, for home.

TEN

Burgled

The next day at school, Mory sat staring at the sky. She had a lot to think about. Yesterday, Sarah's house had been burgled. She had been at the dentist with her mum. The thief had taken Sarah's money box, all her mother's jewellery, some housekeeping money and a valuable clock. How could he? she thought. Thank goodness they'd hidden the necklace.

Absentmindedly tapping her pencil against a finger, Mory realised that finding Royden's hideaway was one thing, stopping him from stealing was another. And worse, Sarah had talked about her mum taking her to the dentist. Mory guessed Lionel had passed the information on.

Her concern about the burglary didn't quite eclipse her joy about Dancer. The pony was turning out to be everything she had hoped and today Bob the farrier was shoeing her for the first time. Mory had wanted to be there but her parents insisted she come to school. She glanced at her watch. The shoes would be on by now.

Thinking of Dancer reminded her of the story she was supposed to be writing. Something exciting. Mrs Wynne had read a piece from *Treasure Island* and they'd discussed why the story was so gripping. Now Mory was trying to make her own story as thrilling. What words should she use? How short or long should the sentences be? How should she describe galloping on Dancer as she had done on the way home yesterday when Dancer went like the wind? She longed to write the excitement down but it was difficult to write down a feeling. She chewed her pencil.

Well, she'd tell it as it happened and hope that would work. She began to write. "It was my first real gallop. It began on a long uphill slope and we were in a hurry. . . " By lunchtime she had finished. Flushed with concentration, she handed her book to Caroline who was collecting them.

The rest of the day passed in a welter of frustration for Mory as her mind raced. Where did Royden hide the things he stole? In his shed or somewhere else? Had he burgled their house while she was at school? Had Dancer minded being shod?

What a relief when the school bus finally dropped them off. Mory sped ahead, running all the way to the Black Rock, straight to the ponies to look at Dancer's four new shoes.

"I bet that feels a bit different," Mory said,

pausing a moment to stroke the pony's inquisitive face. Dancer nuzzled her hand as if to say "A bit". Patting her, Mory hurried indoors, going from room to room. Nothing was different.

She went to see if the cotton was still across the hayloft stairs. It was. Satisfied that all was well, she went to the cowshed in search of David. She found him at his wheel throwing a mug.

"How was school?" he asked, slipping the mug onto a shelf with some others.

"Okay. Was Dancer nervous when Bob shod her?"

"She didn't seem to be."

"Did you hold her?"

"No, Uncle Glyn did. She was very good. Go and take a look."

"I already have," said Mory. "Where's Mum?"

"Teaching."

Mory glanced around. The cowshed was beginning to look more permanent than temporary, she thought. Shelves were up, pots were drying out on them. The kiln was firing and buckets of glaze were everywhere. There was even a brick stand with a sink on it rigged to some plumbing in the yard.

"How are you getting on?" she asked.

"Like a house on fire. If only that flipping concrete would dry out properly, I could start building my big kiln."

David washed his hands and they joined Josh in

the kitchen. David made tea and Mory made some toast while Josh told all about the latest burglary.

"Sarah said whoever it was got in by breaking a window at the back of the house. They did it when she and her mum were at the dentist," said Josh. Mory let out a big sigh.

"Don't worry about us being burgled," said David, noting Mory's expression. "We're too far off the beaten track for anyone to bother."

Famous last words, thought Mory, spreading some peanut butter and wishing she could tell what she knew.

When tea was over, Cara joined them and they rode in the field. Josh and Cara practised jumping. Mory practised obedience and, putting all thoughts of Royden and burglaries to the back of her mind, enjoyed walking and trotting, trotting and walking, trotting and cantering, cantering and trotting. It was totally absorbing.

"Why don't you try a jump, Mory? Just a little one," said Cara.

"I'll start tomorrow," said Mory.

"Scaredy cat," said Josh.

But it wasn't that. It was too soon to ask Dancer to jump and Mory didn't want to ride one of the other ponies, not today, when riding Dancer was so exhilarating that she didn't want to stop.

When they came to untack and wash down their ponies, Mory was grinning with pleasure.

"Dancer's fantastic," she said. "Fantastic – and not one single buck. It's like riding the crest of a wave."

"I thought it was riding a pony," said Josh. Cara laughed. Mory didn't notice the sarcasm or didn't care.

Her euphoria lasted until supper was nearly over. She was miles away when Sheila started to talk about the science teacher vacancy at Aberdawl Comprehensive.

"I think I'll apply," she said. "It's a nice school. You'll see what the staff are like at the party on Saturday." Mory paused in mid mouthful.

"What party?" she asked, coming down to earth with a bang.

"The headteacher's party to which David and I have been invited."

Mory looked at Josh. They both knew this meant putting the necklace back in Sheila's jewellery case. What a blow.

"Did Josh tell you about the burglary?" said Mory, covering up her agitation.

"Don't worry," said Sheila. "It's unlikely to happen to us. We live at the back of beyond."

"That's what Dad said," said Mory. Sheila looked at the two serious faces and laughed.

"Do we look like the sort of people to burgle? We've got practically nothing worth taking."

After the tidying up was finished, Mory and Josh went upstairs, both feeling uneasy.

"I don't like it," said Josh. "I think we should tell Mum and Dad what's happening."

"We can't. I promised Lionel."

"What if we lose the necklace?"

"Look, Mum won't look in the case until she's getting ready. If we bring the necklace in on Saturday afternoon and take it in turns to keep guard, we can hide it again on Sunday."

"I suppose so," said Josh. "I wish the police would catch him."

"He can't be leaving any clues. You need clues to catch a thief."

Over the next few days, Mory's anxiety grew less as nothing further was seen or heard of Royden. Each night after school they rode in the field and Mory did her first jump on Rustler. It wasn't nearly as difficult as she'd thought once she got the idea of folding herself up as the pony jumped. By Friday night, Mory was really looking forward to the riding lesson booked for the following day, so much so that she almost forgot about Royden. It was Josh who reminded her.

"And once we've got the necklace indoors we'll have to guard it all the time."

"Don't worry, Josh, we will," said Mory.

On Saturday morning, Mory was up early. She brought Dancer in and groomed her until her coat gleamed. She combed her mane and went through her tail hair by hair. She was ready ages before the

others, so she nipped to the hayloft stairs and ran her fingers along the cotton to check no one had been up there.

The three of them tacked up their ponies and rode to Llangabby, where Aunt Olwen was waiting with the trailer. Mory hoped they'd all fit in and they did, Rustler and Dancer in the back, Misty in the front.

"There, I told you there'd be no problem," said Uncle Glyn. "It's designed to take three."

They drove off, waving to Uncle Glyn out of the window.

The Spencers' car and trailer were already in the car park when they drove into Penyworlod.

"Looks as if Caroline's going to be with us again," Mory groaned. They unloaded the ponies. Dancer was curious but not nervous and she behaved well when Mory led her round the indoor school behind the others.

"Good girl," she said. "It's a bit strange, eh?"

Caroline was riding Doughnut. No one said anything and neither did she, though she looked a bit sheepish. Dancer worked really hard once she stopped looking at everything. She was at her funniest when asked to go over the trotting poles. She lifted her legs very high and tried to jump them. But Mory persevered and soon she was trotting over them as if she'd done it hundreds of times.

When the others started jumping, Mory watched with Caroline.

"Are you going to have a go?" Mory asked.

"Mind your own business." Mory noticed that Caroline's bottom lip trembled and it occurred to her that Caroline was frightened.

"I find jumping a bit scary," she said, wanting to be of comfort.

"You would."

Mory sighed. It wasn't easy trying to be nice to Caroline.

Misty and Rustler both jumped nicely and Josh

was really getting the hang of it. He offered Mory a go on Rustler.

"Good idea," said Megan. Mory took her courage in her hands and trotted Rustler to a line of jumps. Up and over, up and over, up and over.

"I did it!" She waved a victorious arm, received a round of applause and gave Rustler a thank-you pat.

"Well done," said Megan at the end of the lesson. "You've all improved a lot. And Mory, you've done very well with Dancer."

Caroline sniffed. "She's had lots of help, so it's really not surprising, is it?"

Mory managed to ignore the remark.

It wasn't until they were driving home that Mory remembered the sapphire necklace. Would her mother wear it, she wondered? Whatever she did, it must go back to its drawer in readiness.

Aunt Olwen drove them into the yard at Llangabby, where they unloaded the ponies. Mory gave Dancer lots of pats and a reward for being so good. The pony seemed to have enjoyed her outing and chewed her carrot appreciatively.

"See you this evening," said Aunt Olwen as they rode the ponies down to Black Rock. Aunt Olwen was keeping an eye on Mory and Josh while Sheila and David went to the party. "Come straight back up for lunch, Cara."

They gave the ponies some pony nuts and turned them out in the field. Then Cara went home.

"We'll bring in the you-know-what after lunch," said Mory, nodding towards the barn.

"Okay," said Josh and they made their way indoors.

As soon as the drying up was finished, Mory and Josh went to the barn. They carried the ladder up the hayloft steps, breaking the cotton barrier, and positioned it against the far wall. Josh climbed up and pulled out the stone. He passed the plastic bag to Mory and returned the stone to its place. They left the ladder on the floor and hurried back indoors.

Josh went ahead to make sure their parents' bedroom was empty and stood guard while Mory put the necklace in the case.

For the rest of the afternoon, they took it in turns to watch. Mory checked the bedroom again and again in between trying to draw pictures. It was a relief when her parents began to get ready.

"Are you going to wear your necklace?" Mory asked.

"I don't know," said Sheila. "It's a bit dressy."

"But it's lovely," said Mory.

"Yes, it is. Oh, all right then." Mory did up the clasp. The sapphires sparkled. Finally David and Sheila got in the car and drove off.

The next morning, Mory awoke to the tap tap tap of tiny feet on the roof tiles. A stab of fear swept through her. She went to the window and peeped through the curtains. It was only a pigeon cooing to its mate. Laughing at herself, she dressed quickly and went downstairs to let Splodge out. Then she crept back upstairs to her parents' room and looked in. Both were sound asleep. To her dismay she saw the necklace hanging over the corner of the dressing table mirror. She remembered, with a sinking feeling, that sometimes Sheila left it like that for days. She hoped her mother would put it away later but she didn't.

Mory didn't dare leave the house. All through breakfast she was aware of the necklace hanging unprotected, with the window wide open, airing the room.

"What am I going to do?" she said.

"Just take it," said Josh.

"I can't. Mum'll notice. I'll have to stay and guard it."

"I'd better tell Uncle Glyn I can't help with the sheep," said Josh.

"No, there's no point in both of us staying," said Mory. "You go."

She went to the bedroom to close the window, only to find her mother making the bed.

"Aren't you going riding?" Sheila asked.

"Later."

"You don't sound very keen. Why not come and help Olwen and me make marmalade for the W.I.?" Sheila suggested.

"The Women's Institute!" said Mory. "No thank you. I've got better things to do." She escaped to her room and waited until Sheila drove up the track to Llangabby, desperate to shut the window. She got as far as the landing when David called from the bottom of the stairs.

"Can you spare a few minutes, Mory? I need two pairs of hands." Mory stood in a dither. If she went into the bedroom David would wonder why, but she didn't want to go out until the window was closed. It was such an invitation to a thief. Only a matter of climbing onto the porch roof and stepping inside.

"Mory, are you up there?" David began to climb the stairs.

"Yes, coming," said Mory. She'd have to leave it.

She followed David out to the pottery. She held a piece of boarding in place while David secured it. It seemed to take forever but it couldn't have been longer than ten minutes.

As soon as she could, Mory hurried indoors. On her way upstairs she heard a thud. She ran along the landing and flung open the bedroom door.

The dressing table mirror was knocked forward and the necklace gone. She leapt across the bed to the window which, unsecured, swayed in the breeze. A black-helmeted figure disappeared behind the hedge. Grabbing the window frame she scrambled out, sliding onto the porch roof. Too late – an engine thundered into life. Mory was left to watch helplessly as a red motorbike sped its rider up the track and out of sight.

ELEVEN

The Chase

Mory climbed back into the bedroom as David came out of the yard wanting to see who it was. Tears flooded her eyes. Royden must have been watching them. She imagined him freewheeling the motorbike down the track, hiding it and himself, lying ready to pounce the moment he got the chance. He had outwitted her. Angrily, Mory brushed the tears away. But what was she going to do? She must get the necklace back.

"Stop and think," she told herself. There was no time to find the others. She would ride Dancer to Royden's hideaway. What she was going to do when she got there she couldn't imagine, but go she would. What should she take? A halter? Yes, she'd need to tie Dancer up and bailer twine was always useful. A torch in case she had to go in the cave. Right, she'd take her school rucksack, better not tie it to the saddle in case it upset Dancer, she'd hardly notice she was wearing it. Mory tipped her school things onto the bed and ran downstairs.

"Penknife," she said and ran upstairs again, grabbing it from her table. Downstairs, she jammed on her riding hat, picked up the torch from beside the stove and made for the stables. She put the bag and Dancer's saddle and bridle ready. Had she got everything? Torch and penknife. She collected half a dozen pieces of bailer twine and stuffed them into the bag. She couldn't think of anything else. Mory fetched Dancer. It was all taking ages.

"Come on, girl," she said. Dancer seemed surprised at the haste. Mory pulled the gate closed and trotted Dancer to her stable. Soon Royden would be back at his hideaway. What would he do with the necklace then?

Mory slipped the reins over Dancer's head. With trembling hands she asked Dancer to open her mouth. For the first time the pony put her nose in the air. Mory took a deep breath and relaxed. She rubbed Dancer's cheek.

"Come on, now," she said. Mory slipped the bit in the pony's mouth and put the bridle on. The last thing she wanted to do was upset Dancer. Gently she lowered the saddle and did up the girth. Mory stuffed the halter into the rucksack and pulled it on. She led Dancer from the stable and winced at the sound of metal on stone as they crossed the yard. She tried not to hurry but she didn't want David asking questions, especially as he was suspicious about the motorbike.

Once outside the yard, Mory ran down the track while Dancer trotted beside her. When she was a safe distance away, she slowed to a walk.

"Whoa, Dancer," she said. "Good girl." She did up the girth. Dancer stood like a rock while she mounted and they were off.

"I've got to pace us," Mory told Dancer as they trotted up the sheep track to the ridge. "I mustn't wear you out. Royden thinks he's safe, not knowing I know he's the thief. There's no need to rush."

It was all very well telling herself this. The pressure to regain the necklace was immense. She had to get it back. Cantering along the ridge she wondered how. Royden was hardly going to give it back, even if she asked nicely. She'd steal it. But first she had to find it.

She slowed to a trot as they came onto the ridge and scanned the moor. Nothing but the usual sheep scattered across the heather. She asked Dancer to go on and was surprised when the pony tried to turn for home.

"Come on, girl," Mory said. "I know you haven't been out on your own before but go you must." Mory hammered her legs against Dancer's sides. Sensing Mory's determination, Dancer gave in and went forward. Mory patted her.

"I really need your help," she told the pony. "Now is not the time to try it on."

Mory felt exposed in the open and longed for the forest and the shelter it would give. She urged Dancer forward, not asking for too fast a pace downhill so as not to unbalance either of them.

Dancer surprised her with her surefootedness and they arrived at the forestry gate much quicker than Mory expected. She dismounted, unhooked the chain and led Dancer through, closing the gate behind them. The forest was still, the distant fall of water the only sound to be heard.

Remounting, Mory trotted Dancer along the softer edge of the forestry road, trying her hardest to avoid sharp stones. She slowed when she reached the path to Royden's hideaway. Here she turned Dancer into the trees and led her to a place higher up, where she was well hidden. Pulling off her rucksack, she took out a piece of twine and tied it round a tree, leaving a loop. Putting on Dancer's halter she tied the rope to the twine. She ran up the stirrups and tucked the reins behind them, deciding not to loosen the girth in case she needed a quick getaway. She gave Dancer a handful of pony nuts and a pat.

"Won't be long," she said. The pony whickered after her. "You have a rest," Mory said and hurried on down.

Before coming into the open, Mory checked the road. She counted three and made a dash to the top of the path. Keeping herself hidden as much as she could, she made her way down. Seeing the motorbike gave her a jolt and she hid behind a tree. Royden really was here. From now on she went from tree to rock to tree and, as the sound of the water increased, Mory became a little braver about any noise she made.

There was no one in the clearing. Mory crept on hands and knees towards the shed and, crouching against its timbers, felt it vibrate. Royden was inside. Two planks along the bottom were rotten, so she gave them a tentative prod.

Very gently, Mory pulled away a sliver of wood. It flaked into pieces. Keeping an ear open, Mory rummaged in the bottom of her bag. Undoing her penknife, she picked at the wood until a hole appeared. Looking through, she saw legs. It was such a shock she nearly gasped; Royden squatting beside the tea chest. Carefully, Mory picked at the hole to make it bigger. It took ages and she was scared he'd hear.

Now she had a much better view and could see Royden sitting on the tea chest. Mory lay on the ground and looked up. He had a doorstep sandwich in one hand, from which he took a bite, gazing at something he held in the other. Mory wriggled round to change the angle of her sight line and saw the necklace being played between Royden's fingers as he watched the stones sparkle. He took another bite. Mory sat up. Any moment Royden would finish eating. She had to know where he hid the necklace. It was her only chance of getting it back.

The shed shook. Mory looked through the spy hole in time to see the door swing to. She grabbed her rucksack and, taking precious seconds, scrambled round to look out. Royden was striding across the clearing. She didn't know whether he had the necklace with him or not. She pulled the rucksack onto her back, ready to run.

Royden pushed his way between some branches, going towards the water. Mory, scared to move, knew she had to follow him. She made a mad dash, reached the other side of the clearing and wriggled under the bushes on her tummy. A path led down to the water. Here the air was damp with spray and leafy plants grew from crevices in the rock.

Slowly Mory stood up. Cautiously, she edged

forward onto a rocky promontory. A little way away, the water was an angry swirl where the solid sheet from above hit rock and foamed, before spinning on downstream. Where was Royden? Even if he'd got across the water, the rockface on the far side was too steep to climb.

Instinct made her hide. She crouched behind a rock and peeped out. To her utter amazement, Royden stepped from behind the waterfall as if he were a conjuror stepping from behind a magic curtain. Terrified in case he had seen her, Mory remained glued to her hiding place. She waited in an agony of suspense until she saw him climb the bank and disappear into the bushes.

When she was quite sure he wasn't coming back, she crossed the rocks to the waterfall and found a doorway. Water on one side and rock the other. She stepped through into a cave. Blinking, she took out the torch. It wasn't a deep cave. Treading carefully, she made her way to the back.

She shone the light about her and by luck discovered a smaller cave tucked secretly into the rock. It was a brilliant hiding place. Royden must have thought so too, for a black plastic bag lay on the floor. Mory opened it. Inside was a plastic box and in the box, lots of plastic carrier bags. She picked one from the top of the pile and opened it. At first she thought there was nothing inside until her hand felt a chain. It was the sapphire necklace.

Her heart skipped a beat. She'd got it.

Dropping the bag inside the box with the others, she zipped the necklace into her rucksack. She left the plastic sack as she had found it. Now she had what she wanted she was anxious to get away as fast as possible.

It was difficult to see from behind the screen of water. She did her best to make sure it was safe and darted out, leaping across the rocks. Reaching the bank, she scrambled up and hid in the undergrowth, lying still for a few moments. Then she wriggled forward and looked into the clearing and saw Royden lighting a fire. She'd have to wait. As she did so, there was the long, undeniable whinny of a lonely pony, shrill enough to penetrate the sound of the water. Dancer! Royden heard it too. He stamped on the fire and ran into the shed.

Seizing her opportunity, Mory charged across the clearing and slammed the shed door. There was a cry of rage and the whole shed shook. She snapped the padlock into place. The door wouldn't hold for long but it gave her a chance. Mory ran.

"Dancer," she panted. "It's me. Thank goodness you're still here." The pony whickered a welcome. "We've got to go." Mory untied the halter. Pulling down the stirrups she swung herself onto the pony's back and, ducking down to avoid low branches, rode to the track. So far so good, she thought and turned Dancer for the gate. The pony, only too

pleased to go, set off in an eager trot.

They were nearing the gate when Mory heard the ominous sound of the motorbike. Royden was after her. There was no time to open the gate. Should she hide in the trees? She was cantering now. Ahead was the fence with a stile next to the gate. Not too high. Would she, could she jump it? They were heading straight towards it. Mory felt the pony slow.

"Go on, Dancer, go on. Jump," urged Mory. The pony pointed her ears and surged forward. Mory grabbed hold of Dancer's mane and one, two, three strides and they were in the air. They came down to land with an awful bump. Somehow Dancer picked herself up again and somehow Mory stayed on. She gathered up the reins, which she'd more or less let go, and Dancer cantered on up the path.

"Not quite how I imagined your first jump, Dancer. But well done," puffed Mory, looking back over her shoulder in time to see Royden opening the gate.

The path became steep, impossible to canter, but Dancer trotted fast, twisting and turning round rock and stone. All the time came the sound of the motorbike, screaming and revving, getting closer and closer.

Near the top, where the path was really steep, Mory had to let Dancer walk but the pony, sensing the urgency, put her back into it. This bit was even slower for Royden as the bike slipped on rocky corners and he had to use his legs to keep himself upright.

At last Mory was on the open track. Dancer galloped towards the ridge as fast as she could go but the motorbike sped after her.

The pony couldn't keep this up forever. Mory began to lose hope as the motorbike gained on them. Desperate, she urged Dancer on. Ahead, two riders and a dog appeared, silhouettes on the skyline. It was Josh and Cara with Mab. Mory's spirits lifted. Now she felt she had a chance.

"Go on, girl," she cried. Dancer had seen the ponies too and needed no further encouragement. A whistle sent Mab forward. She raced towards the motorbike. Royden braked as the dog crossed his path. Another whistle and she turned sharply. Royden swerved and must have hit a rock, for the front wheel snapped to the left, sending bike and rider tumbling onto the heather.

"Whoa, girl," said Mory, reining Dancer in. The three riders watched as Royden rose slowly to his feet and lifted the bike. Its front wheel was buckled. Josh whistled and Mab came running towards them, dodging Royden, who aimed a kick.

"Let's go," said Cara.

The three ponies cantered along the ridge, with Mab running at their heels. It wasn't many minutes before they were trotting down the sheep path and clattering into the yard at Black Rock.

"Now we really have got to tell," said Josh.

"Yes," said Mory.

"We guessed something awful had happened when we found you and the necklace were gone," said Cara.

"He stole it but I got it back!"

TWELVE

Caught

"The sapphire necklace was stolen? When?" said David. "But Mory, for goodness' sake, you're crazy. Why didn't you tell me?"

"I promised Lionel." Mory fumbled in her bag. "But I got it back," she said, handing the necklace to her father.

"Attend to that pony," said David. "I'm going to phone Glyn. All three of you are to stay in the yard. I want a full explanation."

Mory led the sweating Dancer into her stable. I'm in for it now, she thought, untacking the pony while Cara fetched water and a sponge. Josh turned the other two ponies out into the field and stroked Mab. He hoped Uncle Glyn wouldn't mind that he'd borrowed his dog.

It wasn't many minutes before Uncle Glyn drove into the yard with Sheila.

"I'm sorry, Uncle Glyn, I would have asked about Mab but you weren't there," said Josh.

"Looks like it's time you had your own dog,"

Uncle Glyn said, opening the Landrover door for Mab to jump in. "The police are on their way."

My own dog! thought Josh, wondering what his parents would say to that. Mory left Dancer to dry off and rest.

"Right," said David. "The whole story please." Mory took a deep breath and told it as quickly as she could, finishing with the most important part.

"We found Royden's hideaway in the forest," she said, "and I know where he hides the stolen things."

"Have you all been there?" Sheila asked.

"Yes," said Mory. "We tracked him."

"Don't ever do anything like it again," David said. "Just think of the danger you've put yourselves in . . ."

Uncle Glyn interrupted.

"Recriminations later," he said. "We must get going."

Everyone piled into the Landrover and Uncle Glyn drove out of the yard and up the track.

"Mory, you guide us. We'll drop Josh and Cara at Llangabby with Sheila. They can show the police the way. Direct them round by the road, mind, Cara. They'll never make it across the hills in a car."

Aunt Olwen was waiting in the Llangabby yard. Those staying piled out to explain and wait for the police. Uncle Glyn drove on.

"What would you do if you were Royden?" Uncle Glyn asked.

"Grab my loot and run," replied David.

"That's what I'd do."

Uncle Glyn turned onto the hills. They drove past the abandoned motorbike; no sign of Royden. Putting the Landrover in four-wheel drive, Uncle Glyn turned downhill. They bumped across the heather, scattering sheep. Mory held tight to the seat and to Mab.

"We wouldn't make it down the stony path," Uncle Glyn said. "Too narrow. The road down here goes straight to the forestry."

They bounced on down with Mory grimly clinging on. At last they reached the road. Uncle Glyn heaved on the steering wheel and they sped to the forestry gate, which David opened. Uncle Glyn waited for David to get back in and drove on.

Mory pointed out the path ahead. Uncle Glyn braked, allowing his passengers to climb out, including Mab, while he backed the Landrover into the trees out of sight.

"In case we're here first. Don't want to warn him off," said Uncle Glyn. Mab stood ready at his heel.

"Stay at the back, Mory," said David.

It was Uncle Glyn and Mab who led the way, David, then Mory, following. Going down was much less scary with her father and uncle for protection. At the edge of the clearing Uncle Glyn waved them back. They took cover just in time. Royden was hurrying towards them, the black plastic bag over his shoulder.

Uncle Glyn whistled and Mab ran forward. Royden lunged at her with the bag; he lunged again, letting the bag go. It caught Mab in the side. Dog and bag rolled over, scattering carrier bags across the clearing. Royden ran. He reached the ivy curtain before Mab was up and scrambled under it. Mab went to follow. A whistle called her off.

"Guard the entrance," shouted Uncle Glyn. "It's a cave."

Uncle Glyn ran up the path, Mab at his heels, leaving David waiting by the ivy.

"Stand by the shed, Mory," David said. Mory did as she was told, wondering where Uncle Glyn had run to and what would happen if Royden came out.

Anxious minutes ticked by when suddenly, Cara, Josh, Sheila, a policewoman and a policeman spilled into the clearing. On their arrival, several stones bounced down the rock face. Everyone looked up. High above, Royden was edging his way along a ledge. He stopped when Mab appeared and blocked his path.

"The game's up, Royden. You come quietly and I'll call the dog off," shouted Uncle Glyn. "You can't get away."

"How do I get up there?" asked the policeman,

not waiting for a reply. The policewoman followed.

For one awful moment, Mory thought Royden was going to jump. Then, realising there was no escape, forward or back, he shuffled along the ledge towards Uncle Glyn and Mab backed away. Royden was caught.

"Royden's in the police car," Uncle Glyn said, when he and Mab joined them. Mory felt a surge of elation until she remembered Lionel. What was going to happen to him? A fit of shivering overcame her but she wasn't really cold.

"Please, don't touch anything," the policewoman said, hurrying into the clearing. Nobody had. "We have to wait for our colleagues from the CID."

"Royden Jones is the thief," said Mory. "He stole the school fund money and Mum's sapphire necklace." Mory felt a choking in her throat and a wobbling in her knees. She sat down to recover.

"I want the whole story," said the policewoman, taking out her notebook.

"From the beginning," said Cara, looking at Mory. Josh nodded. Mory took a deep breath and began, telling how Royden had made Lionel spy for him, how after she had stood up for Lionel outside school, Royden had chased the three of them on his motorbike, how Lionel had told Royden about the sapphire necklace, how they had hidden it and how Royden had stolen it in the end.

"Lionel warned me," said Mory. "But he made

me promise not to tell." The policewoman wrote it all down.

"Don't worry," said Sheila. "Royden won't be able to harm Lionel any more, neither will he be able to steal again. And I have my sapphire necklace, haven't I?" David put his hand in his pocket.

"Here it is," he said, looking thoughtful.

"How did you know about the cave, Uncle Glyn?" Mory asked.

"I used to come here when I was a boy. A tunnel leads up to the ledge. Lucky I knew it, eh? He'd have got away otherwise."

"Did you know about the cave behind the waterfall?"

Uncle Glyn looked surprised.

"No," he said. "I never found that one."

"That's where Royden hides the stolen goods."

"You must show the CID when they get here," said the policewoman.

It was quite late when Uncle Glyn dropped them at Black Rock. They'd waited ages for the detectives and then the whole story had to be told again. Struggling against an overwhelming fatigue, Mory went into Dancer's stable. The pony whickered a greeting.

"Come on," said Mory. "Let's put you out with the others." She led the pony to the field and let her go, watching a moment as the pony put her

head down to graze. Then, with a yawn, she went indoors.

"Mum," she said. "What's going to happen to Lionel?"

"Nothing nasty," said Sheila. "He's a very neglected boy. I'm hoping that now this has happened, the social services will do something to help him."

"But what?"

"Make sure his father takes better care of him."

"But his dad's just like Royden. You saw what he was like that time with the hens."

"Yes, I know, but maybe with help and support from others he can change."

"So Lionel definitely won't have to go to prison or anything?"

"No, he won't."

Mory's mind, set at rest on that count, was still uneasy. Her broken promise rankled and she longed to explain it to him.

"But," said Sheila, "we've really got to get this thing with Caroline Spencer sorted out."

"I have Mum, really," said Mory. "Only once I'd taken the sapphire necklace to school I was done for. If I'd known what would happen, I would never have done it. I really didn't want you to find out because . . ." Mory trailed off.

"Because you knew I'd be cross?"

"Yes, and because I knew I'd been stupid. I'm really sorry, Mum. I won't ever do it again. Mrs Wynne knew I wouldn't. That's why she never said anything. She was really nice about it."

"Oh, Mory, what are we going to do with you?"

"Will I have to be a witness at Royden's trial?" Mory asked, not fancying the idea one bit.

"No, I think there are plenty of adults who can do that. Your statement will be enough. He was caught red-handed, don't forget." Sheila smiled. "I suppose, if I look on the bright side, I've got a heroine for a daughter," she said. "After all, if it wasn't for you, Royden might have got away with everything."

"Well," said Mory, "if this is what being a heroine feels like, I can give it a miss."

Sheila gave her a hug.

"You'll feel better in the morning after a good

night's sleep," she said, which was true.

When Mory woke the following day, she did so with a blissful sense of relief. Splodge was purring on her toes and, as she stretched a long satisfying stretch, he came and rubbed his nose against her chin. She lay there stroking his soft fur; no more worrying about the sapphire necklace; no more anxiety about Royden. What was she going to do today? She sprang out of bed.

"Practise jumping, that's what I'll do," she said, remembering that in all the excitement of yesterday, she had not told a single person of Dancer's amazing jump.

All's Well

"What do you mean, you don't believe it?" said Mory. Having told Sarah about Dancer's amazing jump, Caroline had butted in as usual.

"That pony couldn't possibly jump a stile – it's too green." Mory's mouth fell open. Caroline was the first person who hadn't believed that Dancer had jumped.

"Are you calling my sister a liar?" said Josh. "Are you?"

"I believe Dancer jumped it," said Lionel, blushing to the roots of his hair. He'd just parked his bicycle and was hovering on the edge of the group, listening.

"Lionel!" said Mory. "I've got to talk to you."

"I don't think you should. He's got a thief for a brother," said Caroline.

"Shut up," said Mory and took Lionel to one side. "I had to tell everything to the police. Nothing's going to happen to you. Mum says so. You'll be all right."

"My dad went mad when the police came," said Lionel. "I hid. Swearing and raving. Going on about how he knew Royden'd go to the bad. I'm staying away after last night. Till he cools off. If he finds out what I told, I've had it."

"Where will you go?"

"I got somewhere."

"Come home with us." Lionel shook his head.

"Couldn't," he said. "What would your mam say?"

"She'd understand." Lionel shook his head again.

"No, ta," he said. "I know where to go."

Mory didn't pursue it and when the bell rang and they went into school, she found herself something of a celebrity. News of Saturday's events had travelled fast.

"Mory got my parents' clock back and Mum's jewellery," said Sarah. There was a clamour for Mory to tell the whole story and she did her best.

"Sounds like a pack of lies to me," said Caroline.

"Don't be stupid," said Sarah. "It's true. My parents rang the police to find out."

Mrs Wynne clapped her hands and, like all excitement, it died down once the day got underway. It wasn't until the English exercise books were given out that Mory's exploits were mentioned again.

"You wrote well, Mory," Mrs Wynne said. "And now you have an even more exciting story to tell." Mory blushed.

"See," whispered Sarah. "Told you it was true." Caroline sniffed and didn't speak to anyone for ages.

At home time when they were putting on their coats, Sarah suddenly remembered to ask if they were entering the Penyworlod Show.

"You bet," said Cara.

"So am I," said Sarah. "I've got to get practising."

"Practise with us," said Mory.

"Don't tell me you're entering," said Caroline.

"Of course I am," said Mory. "Aren't you?"

"Lionel's riding my pony," said Caroline. "That's because he's the best rider round here. He'll win everything, of course." There was a general groan. Lionel overheard, blushed scarlet and hurried out.

"Lionel, wait," said Mory. He wouldn't. He ran across the playground, grabbed his bike and was gone.

"Have you asked him?" said Mory.

"He'll jump at the chance to ride Tawney, don't you worry," said Caroline.

"I'm surprised you'd let a thief's brother sit on your precious pony," Mory said and stomped off to wait for the bus.

"Poor Lionel," said Cara, joining her.

"He'll be all right," said Mory. "He loves riding Tawney. Caroline's worth putting up with for that. But his dad might not let him."

"Jumping practice when we get back," said Josh.

"Yes," said Mory.

She was looking forward to it after yesterday, when jumping Dancer in the field had been a great success. At first Misty and Rustler had given her leads. Dancer happily jumped everything they jumped. Then she had jumped on her own but nothing as big as the stile. It would be a long time before Mory asked anything like that of Dancer or herself again. Thinking back, she was staggered that she had dared. Now it was like a secret. She knew that Dancer could do it and one day would do it again.

Lionel wasn't at school the next day or the next, so it wasn't until Thursday that Mory saw him again. He came into the playground looking like a different person. He actually smiled when Mory said hello.

"Where've you been?" she asked.

"Lying low," said Lionel.

"Is everything all right with your dad?"

"Yes," said Lionel. "It is." And that was all he said. Try as she would, he said nothing else. Lionel shut tight like a clam.

Later that evening, Mory found out what had happened. It was Cara who brought the news. She had telephoned Megan Reece to book them a riding lesson.

"Megan asked if Lionel was in school today. I said yes, but that he had been away for two days.

She said she knew that and just wanted to make sure that today he'd turned up. Then she asked to speak to Mum," said Cara.

"Go on," said Mory.

"She and Mum had this long conversation. It went on for ages."

"About Lionel?"

"Ian found him asleep at the back of the hay barn on Tuesday morning and there was a terrible row about it with the people who look after children at the council."

"With Ian? It wasn't his fault."

"No, with Mr Jones. He hadn't even bothered to report Lionel missing. Anyway, it seems that he, Mr Jones that is, has had a telling off about looking after Lionel and Megan and Ian have arranged for him to stay at Penyworlod every weekend."

"And Mr Jones said yes?"

"It looks like it."

"No wonder Lionel was so cheerful this morning," said Mory. "That's really good news."

"The photographs have come," said Josh, bursting in. "They're really good. Do you want to see them?"

"Yes, please," said Mory. She looked at them carefully. "They're super, especially the ones of Dancer." Josh let her choose one to keep.

"I'll put it on the wall," said Mory. "Thanks, Josh, that's great."

Later Mory asked Sheila if she could phone Hannah.

"I want to tell her everything that's happened," said Mory.

"Don't be on the phone for ever," said Sheila. "That's all I ask."

It was great to hear Hannah's voice and Mory spent much longer than she meant telling her the news. Hannah was astounded the country was so exciting.

"I can't wait to come," she said. "And guess what? I'm having my first riding lesson next Saturday."

"Fantastic," said Mory. "You wait. The riding here is out of this world."

Mory went to bed full of enthusiasm for life. She tickled Splodge and stroked his ears. Everything had turned out better than she could ever have hoped. In three weeks it would be half term and the Penyworlod Show. She was really looking forward to it. She and Dancer would work very hard, and, who knows, might even enter for the jumping. Mory curled up under her duvet and imagined it all until she fell fast asleep.